Sweetest Taboo

A novel

By

Eva Márquez

*To a young soul who left this
world far too soon
and whose beauty and spirit touched
and inspired those who knew her.*

Table of Contents

Preface..vii

Chapter One: Careless Whisper 1

Chapter Two: It's Raining Men, Hallelujah!................................ 7

Chapter Three: Is it a Crime? 23

Chapter Four: Sowing the Seeds of Love 33

Chapter Five: Sweetest Taboo 49

Chapter Six: More than Words...59

Chapter Seven: Friday, I'm in Love 69

Chapter Eight: Winds of Change...89

Chapter Nine: It Ain't Over 'til It's Over.................................. 111

Chapter Ten: No More "I Love You's" 127

Chapter Eleven: I'll stand by You... 137

Chapter Twelve: Better Be Home Soon..................................... 149

Chapter Thirteen: Believe 159

Chapter Fourteen: Why Does My Heart Feel So Bad?.......... 165

Chapter Fifteen: Losing My Religion....................................... 177

Chapter Sixteen: Come What May.. 193

Chapter Seventeen: No Ordinary Love 205

Chapter Eighteen: Sweet Surrender... 213

Chapter Nineteen: Into Temptation.. 219

Chapter Twenty: Just Like Heaven.. 233

Chapter Twenty-One: It's the End of the World
as We Know It... 239

Chapter Twenty-Two: With or Without You 251

Chapter Twenty-Three: Please, Please Tell Me Why?........... 257

Chapter Twenty-Four: You Were Meant for Me..................... 267

Epilogue 283

Preface

Dear Reader,

My story begins in the early 90s when a young girl started her high school career. She may have been any girl – young, impressionable, and fresh into the wide world of older boys, harder classes, and more choices. She may have been quite beautiful, well developed for her age, and smarter than most of the other students in her class. She may have been destined for the same high school career as anyone else – honors courses, braces, a few high school crushes, photography classes, a first kiss, and then a straight shot into the college of her choice, and her future as a doctor, or teacher, or architect.

Instead, she fell in love with her swim coach, one of the most popular teachers in the school, and became romantically involved with him.

I don't believe that I have to tell you how dangerous this would have been. She was a young girl of 15, 16, 17 and he an adult man in his late 30s, old enough to be her father. Although this type of relationship would have passed as acceptable and even normal in Medieval England, the modern world frowns on such dalliances, and prosecutes the men

- and women - who take advantage of adolescent students in this way. The two of them, then, would have been facing the threat of discovery, tarnishing of reputation, and even time behind bars; throwing their relationship in the face of society, if you will, but doing so quietly, in order to avoid detection.

Have you guessed, yet, that the story I'm telling you is true? Have you guessed that it's more than just a rhetorical question, more than an idea that developed in my head one day?

The girl in the story is my mother, Isabel Cruz. She never told her story to the world, though she could have, because she didn't want her love and relationship to be tainted by society's judgments. This was a story of an illicit - and illegal - love. It was a story of lying, cheating, and misleading the authorities. My mother's love for this older man was forbidden, and would have been highly scandalous to the world at large. She might have lost privileges, opportunities, and even her family, had they found out. And for him … his future and very life would have been put in jeopardy if the nature of their relationship were revealed, regardless of whether my mother sought to prosecute him or not. Even when she was older, my mother feared that the truth about their relationship might bring a backlash to the man she had loved so dearly. She fought against that with all her might, with the ongoing wish to keep him from any risk or pain. She never lost her love for him, scandalous as it may have seemed to others.

She is older, now, and the man in the story is long gone. When I happened across her diary from that time and asked her permission to write the story, she acquiesced. It was time that the world knew, she said, so it could see that this type of love - though it may be frowned upon, and even prosecuted - isn't always what it seems. Sometimes, regardless of the ages of the participants, it is just that. Love. True and pure as it can be between two people, and strong enough to last through the years. It was time, she said, for our family to know its past, and its future.

I have just closed her diary, having squeezed every word from it, and written my own last words, which means that the book is done and her story has been told. I must pass it to you now, Reader, and trust you to hold it dear and keep it safe. I must trust you to see the love that shines through, rather than the social mores of the situation. I must trust you to care for my mother and her past, as I have during the writing of this book.

This, then, is my mother's story. It starts when she was very young, only 15 ...

~ Claire Stevens

Chapter One

Careless Whisper

$\mathcal{B}$y my calculations, I had seven minutes. I had to make my move right now, or it would be too late.

I strained my ears and listened for my brother's deep voice whispering down the hall. He always ended the conversations with his girlfriend with a "good night" and "I love you." But there was nothing. Silence. I frowned. I knew my parents were already asleep; I could no longer hear their pillow talk - the steady murmurs that used to comfort me when I was a kid - from the other side of the wall. At least that meant I was safe to go looking.

I left my bedroom and crept down the empty hall, but didn't find my brother. I moved through the house stealthily, switching off the ringers to all three telephones. I went first to my mom's office, next in the kitchen, and finally to the living room, where I found the cordless phone's cradle empty. I switched the ringer off quietly, then looked around the room.

Tony still had the cordless phone. He usually returned it to its cradle after he said goodnight to Amy. What was he doing? Was he expecting another call? Was he keeping the phone out of spite? I gulped down my frustration and fear. He could ruin everything. Worse, he could catch me and turn me in. I thought I still had about five minutes to find the phone and get outside, though.

I crept barefoot down the hallway, a cold chill running down my back. Tony's bedroom door was ajar, the flickering lights of the TV slanting into the darkened hallway from his room. I tiptoed toward the door and peered through the gap.

I was relieved at what I saw. My brother had fallen asleep with the TV on and the phone in hand. The idiot. Tonight, of all nights. I sucked in a deep breath, stretched out my hand, and pushed the door open. The hinge let out a slight creak and I froze. The loud groans of our old house were the last thing I needed right now. I waited until the door stopped moving, and listened intently for any other sound. Nothing. No one was awake but me.

I held my breath, pushed the door a little wider, and slipped into the room. The carpet was thick under my feet, cushioning my quiet footsteps as I padded closer to my brother's sleeping form, while my nerves fired with every step. I was terrified of being caught, but I needed that phone like I needed to breathe. I held my breath and reached out slowly, pulling the phone from Tony's hand.

Tony stirred, mumbled something, and turned over with a grunt.

I didn't breathe again until I was out of the room and rushing toward the kitchen. I glanced at the clock as I passed and exhaled; three minutes to spare. I crept across the living room, the phone held tightly in my fist, and took a wide path around the coffee table. The last thing I needed right now was to crash into something and wake the whole house. Luckily, the full moon's warm light shone through the mini blinds in the living room, casting a glow across everything in the room.

I turned the brass knob on the kitchen door with a light touch and tiptoed out to the patio. The phone would ring any minute. I swung the door almost shut behind me, but left it slightly ajar; as to not make any noise when I went back inside. The night air surrounded me, invigorating me with its touch and promise of dark corners and secrets. The wind blew through my hair on its way to the gigantic maple tree at the far end of our backyard, where it rushed across the dry leaves. This was good – the sound of the leaves would conceal the sound of my voice. I sat cross-legged on the cool patio floor, and wondered nervously if the buzz of the cordless phone would wake anyone inside. It never had before, but there was a first time for everything.

This wasn't the first night I'd sat barefoot on the patio, cordless phone in hand. I'd sat out here like this many nights, and it always made me feel … alive. Even with the dim light of the full moon, the other side of our yard was dark. Mysterious. Full of possibility. Of course I knew that during the day there was a fence there to keep the neighbor's horses out and our little terrier in. At night, though, in the dark, the whole world seemed somehow larger.

The cool spring breeze found its way under my long hair and I wished that I was wearing my favorite flannel shirt instead of the fitted pink tank top I had on. I shivered, staring at the darkness of our yard, and thought suddenly of the rapist and murderer who had terrorized our community when I was younger. My father had put special locks on our doors and windows, and no young girls had been allowed out after dark. I had been too young to really understand, but it had left a lingering mark. How did I know there wasn't some nutcase just over the fence, waiting for a moment like this, when he could to jump out and assault a seventeen-year-old girl in her tank top and shorts?

The phone vibrated suddenly and my heart jumped, startling me out of my morbid thoughts. I pressed the green *Talk* button on the phone, a lump forming in my throat.

"Tom?" I asked in a hoarse whisper, my stomach full of butterflies. It was still a little strange to call him by his first name, even after all these years. Especially when everyone else at Royal Oaks High called him "Mr. Stevens."

"Isabel," came the familiar voice. "How are you?" His voice was gentle and deep. It soothed me instantly, the same way it had when I was fifteen. There was an edge to his voice tonight, though, and I sensed that there was something bothering him.

"Is something wrong?" I asked. I didn't want to admit that I already knew exactly what it was; my high school graduation was coming up. It would bring an end to our current arrangement. We hadn't talked about our future yet, but I had known that it was coming.

After a few pensive moments, Tom spoke.

"You're my sweetheart," he told me, his voice sad. "I can't imagine life without you. I don't want to have to imagine life without you."

Tom rarely used terms of endearment with me, these days. When he did – in these rare moments when he called me his sweetheart – my heart melted. All of the turmoil, the sleepless nights, the protracted nature of our relationship, became nothing more than a passing inconvenience and very worthwhile. Tonight, though, I knew that the word came with drawbacks. They gave me the courage I needed to say the words I'd been dreading.

"My graduation won't affect our relationship, you know that," I told him. "Look at how much we've been through together. If we made it through all of that, we can make it through anything. Tom, I want to be with you always, no matter where life takes me after graduation."

I spoke passionately, fully believing in what I said. I was absolutely devoted to this man. But somewhere deep inside, I knew I was being dishonest. Neither of us wanted our relationship to change, but it was clear that things *were* going to change, and soon. I had just been offered a place at a small, private liberal arts college on the East Coast. The choice had been difficult because although I wanted to stay close to Tom, I also wanted to move forward with my life. In the end, I accepted the offer. Tom hadn't really reacted when I told him. It hadn't affected our relationship. Now, though, the cracks were starting to show.

"I want to believe that," Tom answered quietly. "I loved the last letter you wrote me. Every time I read your letters, I feel like I'm sixteen again. I feel like I've come out of a deep sleep." A pause, and then, "I can't lose you, Isabel. You're the reason I wake up in the morning; I can't love anyone more than I love–"

Suddenly I heard a distinct *click* on the line. My heart plummeted.

"Did you hear that?" Tom snapped, his tone suddenly terse. "Did someone pick up the phone at your house?"

"Hold on a minute, let me check inside." I slipped back inside and listened, but the house was completely quiet. The kitchen phone was on the counter, my mom's office was dark, and I was holding the only other phone in the house.

"Who picked up the phone?" Tom repeated, worry coloring his voice.

The *click* had not originated on my end of the line. I should've been relieved, but my panic rose even more.

"Tom," I whispered into the receiver. "It wasn't here, everyone's asleep..."

"I have to go," Tom interrupted abruptly. "Danielle's coming."

There was another click, and the line went dead.

Chapter Two

It's Raining Men, Hallelujah!

My freshman year of high school had been ... empowering. I'd found it almost immediately to be a welcome change from the awkwardness of middle school; my friends and I were growing up, we were having good times, and – best of all – the boys that I'd always noticed had finally started noticing me. I'd always been a family-oriented girl, but this new atmosphere brought a new independence, and I'd enjoyed every second of it. I was fourteen and ready for the world and ready for my first relationship with a boy. That year, and the summer after, had become a blur of new boys: Alfredo, Ryan, Brian, David, Charles, Eric ... I felt as though I'd spent my entire life in a box, and was just now finding my way out of it. I never fell in love, though, and I was always careful to stop things before they got too serious. Nothing more than kissing; my parents had raised me to be a respectable girl, and I fully expected to be a virgin at my wedding.

When I started my sophomore year, though, everything changed.

I walked slowly down the open halls of the campus on the first day of sophomore year, reveling in the feeling of being back. The summer had been wonderful, and I'd had a great time, but school still held the things that were important to me - learning, my future, and the daily social interactions. Nothing had changed since the year before, aside from my status in the school. The lockers were still old, rusty, and badly in need of maintenance, though they were decorated today with purple and silver *welcome* signs, in honor of the first day of school. I laughed at the posters; they were hung haphazardly with silver duct tape, and had obviously been done in a hurry. The rest of the school looked exactly the same; drab brown and tan walls, concrete floors, and single-story classroom buildings. The best thing about this particular campus was that it was open to the sky; when I was outside of class, I could lie on the benches or grass lawns, watching the clouds float through the sky, and dream about the future.

I strolled past the window of one of the administrative offices, and glanced subconsciously at the reflection. I'd worn shorts, t-shirts, and jeans during my freshman year, and had been content to look like a tomboy. I was a sophomore now, though, and wanted to look the part, so I'd convinced my mom to buy me a new wardrobe over the summer: skirts, fitted jeans, and tops that showed off my emerging figure. I knew that I was maturing more quickly than some of the other girls in the class, and I intended to take full advantage of it. I'd also been told that I looked like Natalie Wood, and had done my hair in her signature style this morning – pulled back into a high, swinging ponytail, which just brushed the top of my shoulders. The only thing that spoiled my looks were the metal braces on my teeth, but I'd dealt with that. I had spent two full days in front of the mirror over the summer, learning to smile with my lips slightly parted.

I was convinced that this was going to be my year.

I'd even joined the swim team this year, with my best friends Vicky and Natalie, to pad my resume and get the extra-curricular experience. I'd never swum competitively, so it was going to take some work, but it would give me the opportunity to improve my form, enjoy my friends, work on my tan, and catch the eye of boys, who hung around the pool watching us girls in swimsuits.

I smiled shyly at my reflection on the window, then turned and walked away. *Enough daydreaming*, I lectured myself. If this was going to be my year, I needed to start by getting to my first class.

9

By the time January rolled around, swim practice had become the highlight of my day. It gave me something to work toward, and a break in the routine that was my life. It was also an additional activity on my transcript, and I was keenly aware that colleges would be looking for such things when reviewing my application.

I spent most of my time in class looking forward to the last bell. When it sounded, my team members and I rushed to the girls' locker room – dimly lit by just a few fluorescent lights – to change into our suits and do our stretches. I became addicted to the smell of the chlorine, which never left my suit, and the cool, shocking plunge into the refreshing water. The afternoons were warm, even in January, so we always had a crowd of observers. I loved the spectators, and the knowledge that they'd come to see us perform.

Of course, there was something else that sent me rushing to the pool every day. Something bigger and more important than the smell of the chlorine, the cool water, or even the eyes of the audience. Two of our swim instructors were female coaches from the PE department. They handled the beginners and coached the JV team. They also ran the majority of our practices.

The varsity coach, though, was the reason I sprayed on *Exclamation*, my favorite perfume, every afternoon before heading to the pool. Mr. Stevens was the head coach, though he took a back seat to the two assistant coaches during practice. He didn't give us our drills or correct our mistakes, as the two women did. He sat in the shadows instead, watching, and murmuring an occasional comment to one of the assistants. When it came time to separate into different teams, he took the varsity team to the smaller pool to work with them. I'd never had a personal conversation with him, and I didn't know if he'd ever even looked at me.

That, of course, just made me even more attracted to him. I'd always had crushes on older men, but Mr. Stevens was the most attractive man I'd ever seen. Tall, athletic, broad-shouldered ... he had the short dirty-blonde hair and hazel eyes that I'd always found very attractive, with deeply tanned skin and full, pouting lips. I had never noticed him before I joined the swim team, but couldn't keep my mind off him once I'd seen him. A bit of quick research told me that he was a teacher as well, and taught both mathematics and photography to the upper classmen in the school. Several of my older friends were taking his class, though they thought I was crazy when I told them I wanted to meet him. None of my friends found him particularly attractive – he was in his late thirties and sporting some gray on his temples, and wasn't exactly a high school jock. I ignored their opinions, though, and embraced my crush with all the fierceness of a love-struck fifteen-year-old girl.

I made it my mission in life to meet him and get to know more about him.

"So I hear that Robby Herrera is really into you," Sarah said suddenly, breaking into my thoughts.

I gasped and blinked, clearing my head of the daydream I'd been having, and looked over at her. "What?" I asked gruffly. "Who?"

Sarah pursed her lips in disapproval and followed my eyes to the edge of the green, where Mr. Stevens stood talking to some teachers. "Robby Herrera," she repeated. "You know, he's a student here? He's a freshman, but he seems like a nice guy." She paused, frowning. "Better than having a crush on a creepy teacher," she added darkly.

I narrowed my eyes at her in response. Sarah was the only one who reacted this way to my crush. I assumed that it had something to do with her family life, which wasn't pleasant, but I never took well to being lectured. "You don't know what you're talking about, Sarah," I muttered.

She huffed, crossing her arms. "What's wrong with you?" she snapped. "Do I have to paint a few gray hairs on Robby's head just so you'll give him a chance? Izzy, Mr. Stevens is old enough to be your dad. He's married and has kids. Daughters, not that much younger than us! What are you going to do, become a home wrecker?" She looked at me and shook her head. "I don't know why I even bother. It's not like you even listen to me." She turned and stormed away from the green top toward the classrooms.

I sighed; I didn't know why it meant so much to Sarah, and I didn't know how to make it any better with her. She was right, though - her words had no bearing on my obsession with Mr. Stevens. What she didn't know - though is that I'd been obsessing about it for a week - was that my crush had become even deeper the previous Monday. Mr. Stevens had finally started paying attention to me. I don't know why it happened, or what I had done to attract his eyes, but when I got out of the pool he was standing on the deck, waiting, with my turquoise beach towel in his hand.

That's when I'd known that this crush wasn't as one-sided as I had thought.

He hadn't been waiting for anyone else. He hadn't even said anything to anyone else on the JV team. And he certainly didn't know where anyone else's towel was (this part might have been an assumption on my part). But he knew who I was, and he was waiting for me.

I stared up at him, my mouth open, and my mind raced through all of the implications. First, the fact that he handed *me* the towel, and not anyone else on the team, meant that he was sharing this connection with me, and *only* with me. Second, the fact that Mr. Stevens knew which towel was mine meant that he had been observing *me*. All of this time, when it had seemed to me that he'd never even looked my way, he had been watching. Watching for long enough to know which towel I picked up, at least. And he must have been watching me carefully to know that I always put my bag on the concrete bench near the south end of the pool. He'd known where to look for my towel, and that brought me to my third - and most important - conclusion. He knew when I got to practice, and where I put my things. That must mean that he watched for me to arrive. I took the towel and turned without speaking, dizzy with excitement. I don't know how I made it to the girl's locker room without trip-ping over myself.

After that, things changed.

Three weeks later, we had our first swim meet. This marked the first time that our team would compete together, and the first time we would face a real school in the races. I was ridiculously nervous the night before the meet – would we be badly beaten, or were we as good as we thought we were? I chewed every one of my fingernails during the long day, but finally found myself in my last class. The swimmers were dismissed early and I walked to the girls' locker room with two of my teammates. We gathered our gear from our lockers and headed to the parking lot to wait for the bus. When the yellow school bus arrived, everyone piled in, choosing their preferred seats as they walked the aisle.

"An old bus today," Natalie muttered. "You'd think they could at least offer us a nice bus. We're representing the school, after all."

I shrugged, looking up at the peeling paint and faded let-tering of the bus. "I guess they're doing what they can. Not a lot of money to be had, you know." My eyes traveled over the windows until I found the swim coaches. They were sitting in the front row, as usual.

My lips turned up in a grin and my voice rose. "Anyhow," I continued, "at least we're getting out of school early. And going on a trip."

Natalie turned to me, frowning, then caught the direction of my eyes and grinned back. "And what's got you in such a good mood, Izzy?" she asked, teasing. "Why so excited? It wouldn't be the fact that we're going on a trip ... with Coach Stevens, would it?" She poked me in the ribs and laughed when I squirmed.

"Quiet, you," I laughed. "No one's supposed to know about that!"

Natalie laughed, then grabbed our friend Vicky and climbed up the stairs to the bus. Most of the team chose to sit at the back of the bus, to be as far away from the coaches as possible. My friends and I chose to sit in the row behind them, though, so we could look over their shoulders at the swim assignments. I knew that the two female coaches disliked me – they spent most of their time in practice assigning me extra laps – but sitting behind them would give us an idea of who was swimming what at the meet. Besides, Natalie and Vicky were returning swimmers, and some of their favorites, so the coaches were nice to me when they were around. I glanced past the two women to the other side of the row as we sat down, seeing that Coach Stevens sat by himself, with a list of assignments in front of him.

He looked lonely, I thought, and wondered if he would like some company. The thought of sitting so close to him made me blush, though, and I ducked my face toward the window before anyone could see he color rising in my cheeks.

He'd been friendlier since the towel incident, and people had started to make comments. He was always laughing at my antics now, and had even directed a joke or two my way. I'd turned around to find his remarkable hazel eyes on me more than once, and had learned to smile back when we made eye contact.

Thinking about sitting beside him on the bus was a whole new thing, though, and I didn't think I was quite ready for that.

Natalie, who sat beside me, leaned closer and breathed quietly in my ear. "Why don't you go sit next to your boyfriend, Mr. Stevens." She laughed when I jumped, and I reached out to smack her on the arm.

"Oh stop," she muttered, still smiling. "I can't help it if you're so transparent. I can tell exactly what you're thinking every time you look at him. You need to learn to hide it better."

I shrugged again, grinning, and turned back to the window. She was right. Whatever this was between us, I didn't want to mess it up. And I certainly didn't want it to end. I had to learn to play it cool and blow things off, the way the older girls did. It would never do for people to start suspecting that more was going on - it might ruin things for both of us. Not that anything *was* going on, I reminded myself. Nothing had happened.

At least, not yet.

That didn't change the fact that I wanted to know more about this man. I wanted to know him better, and learn what made him tick. What made him smile, and what made him dream. I wanted to know everything about him: his strengths, his weaknesses, the things that upset him, his fears, what brought him peace ... most of all, I wanted to know all about his desires. And what he thought of me.

I stole another quick glance in his direction and found his eyes on me, his face unreadable. I blushed and looked down quickly, but not before Natalie elbowed me in the side again.

Learn to control your reactions, I reminded myself quietly. *Don't give yourself away so easily.*

The bus had arrived at the unfamiliar high school, nearly thirty minutes away from our campus, before I could work up enough courage to look at Mr. Stevens again. I looked out the window and noted how beautiful the campus was; clean walkways, bright green lawns, and a range of tall, mature trees. The buildings were larger than those at my school, and constructed of colorful red brick. It gave the entire school an established, classic feel, and I smiled to myself. I'd been to several other high schools over the years, and they were always far nicer than ours. The buildings were larger, the trees were more beautiful, and the grass was always greener. There were a number of reasons for the difference – our school was in a low-income part of town, and the students were almost all immigrants or minorities. There wasn't a lot of funding for renovations or even adequate maintenance. It always made me wonder, though. What did the other students think when they came to our school? Did they think we were less than them? Did they wonder if we were some kind of ghetto school?

Did it ever occur to them that we might be just as talented as they were – even better – but without all the fancy trappings?

I squared my shoulders, putting these thoughts away, and focused on the coming meet. We may not have a big, fancy swimming pool like this school did, but I had faith in our team. We had weapons they had never seen and talented, motivated coaches.

I stole a last glance at Coach Stevens, who hadn't looked up again, then stood and walked off the bus with my friends. Our job started now - find the locker rooms, change into our suits, and enter the water to warm up for the competition. Natalie and Vicky had been here before, and walked confidently toward the pool area. As we came around the corner behind them, I heard one of the other girls gasp in surprise. A rich school indeed – they had an Olympic-sized swimming pool in their own back yard. It sat in the midst of a neatly landscaped garden, complete with rolling lawns and a small park-like area for relaxing in "nature." This was the first time I had ever seen such a large swimming pool. I resolutely closed my mouth on my surprise, though, and vowed to show the students of this other school that we were good enough for their pool too.

"Come on, girls," I muttered to my teammates, nudging them toward the nearby locker rooms. We filed into the bright, clean rooms and slipped into our competition suits for the warm-up. These suits were new, and still much tighter than our practice suits. "Tighter suits make for less drag," Natalie had told me at the start of the season. "Always order the smallest suit you can, then suck your gut in to get it on." I breathed deeply, feeling the stretch of the spandex around my ribs, and grinned at the girl next to me. The suits were tight, which meant that they fit us like a second skin.

It also gave everyone else a better look at what we had to offer.

Mr. Stevens hadn't seen me in my new suit before, and I paused before the mirror in the bathroom. Although it was new, the swim suit was already showing wear, but it reflected enough of my body for me to realize that Natalie had been right – this suit was tighter than anything I'd ever worn, and verged on indecent.

"Isabel, where are you? We're warming up!" Vicky shouted through the door. The girl was 5-foot-nothing, but had the loudest voice on the swim team. I could never figure out where she stored all that sound when she wasn't using it.

"I'm coming, I'm coming," I called. I took one more glance in the mirror. "Time to perform," I said firmly. Lifting my chin a notch, I squared my shoulders, turned, and strolled out into the sun.

Coach Stevens and Vicky were waiting for me outside of the girl's locker room. As soon as Vicky saw me, she gave me a nod and ran ahead toward the swimming pool, leaving Mr. Stevens and me to walk alone. This should not have been an awkward moment for either one of us; he was my coach and I was a swimmer on his team. Time spent alone before a meet should have consisted of some last words of wisdom or encouragement. Perhaps we would have discussed the races I was to swim, and my chances against the other team. We may also have talked about the classes he taught, and whether I would be using them to pad my transcript in the next two years.

Instead, though, we said nothing, and the thirty seconds it took us to walk to the poolside were slow and tense. I searched for words that would break the silence, but came up with nothing. This was the chance I had been waiting for - Mr. Stevens was walking next to me, with no one else around. I could have said anything I wanted. But my mind stubbornly refused to tick, and my lips remained glued together.

I noticed instead the confident momentum of his walk, and the proximity of his body to mine. He was close to me - almost close enough to graze my hand with his own. Certainly closer than he should have been. He seemed to tower over me, although he was only about 6 inches taller than I was. That height comforted me; I felt protected in his presence.

He must have felt the awkwardness of the silence, too, because he stopped walking and turned toward me. I stopped in turn and looked up at him.

"Isabel, are you nervous?" he asked quietly.

I had been so preoccupied with my thoughts and fantasies that I replied without thinking. "No, you don't make me nervous."

He drew back, confused, and I felt my cheeks flush crimson. I had misread the situation, and grasped for a way to save the conversation.

"Um, what I mean is, are you trying to make me nervous about my event?" I asked quickly, smiling. "If you are, it's not working," I forced another bright smile and ducked my head, looking up at him through my lashes.

He laughed and placed his hand on the back of my neck, pressing his fingers softly to my skin. I stopped breathing, reveling in the feel of his fingertips caressing me. He leaned forward to speak closer to my ear.

"You've got nothing to be nervous about, young lady. And you certainly don't need to be nervous about me."

I blushed again, and he released me. He had understood my statement, then, and seen through my attempt to cover the mistake. I looked up at him and smiled, then turned and walked toward the pool. As I put my cap on, though, I turned to look at him again, and caught the smile that lingered at the corner of his mouth. My heart hammered at my ribcage and my knees grew weak, but I forced myself to turn away and focus on the upcoming meet.

Chapter Three

Is it a Crime?

Within a couple of months, I had settled into my role on the swim team and started making more friends outside of my normal circle. Liz, a girl in my English and History classes, became one of my closest confidantes, and I started to think of her as the sister I'd never had. She was not on the swim team; in fact, Liz was not involved in any sports at all. She was a tall, boisterous, and slightly chubby Mexican-American, and shied away from any sporting activities. She still stopped by swim practice every day, though, to boost our spirits and crack one or two jokes with us before she headed home. On slow days, she sat on the concrete benches and waited for practice to end. Her house was warmer and friendlier than mine, since she had no siblings that could bother us, and I enjoyed going there after school to do homework or watch TV and eat with her family. I only got to do so on the days when she waited for me. It always warmed my heart to see her sitting on the benches, reading a book and waiting for me to finish with practice.

Mr. Stevens enjoyed her presence as well, and would sometimes sit with her during practice. She was a happy, funny girl, and he enjoyed her sarcastic jokes and unbelievable stories. By the end of the first month of swim season, they'd become friends, and she was making the most of it. She included me in their conversations whenever she could, though that would quickly lead to her being cut out of the conversation. I was always anxious for a reason to talk to Mr. Stevens, and he seemed equally happy to sit with Liz or me. Liz was the only friend who didn't judge me or criticize my crush on Mr. Stevens, a much older man who had a gold wedding band on his finger. She would get Mr. Stevens and I talking, then give me a knowing look and walk quietly away, to wait for me near the entrance of the girls' locker room.

My crush on Mr. Stevens began to rule my teenage world, and keeping track of all our seemingly trivial interactions became an obsession. To be fair, Mr. Stevens hadn't done anything inappropriate at that point, and treated me with the same respect he exhibited to all other swimmers. I believed that he stood closer to me and looked at me with a different look in his eyes, but that might have been my imagination.

In my more rational moments, I was forced to admit that my relationship with Mr. Stevens only existed in my head. Nothing had actually happened. That didn't stop me from feeling a rush of nervous energy every time he came near. And that nervous energy was enough to fuel my crush.

Eventually I became braver. My jokes took a more inquisitive and probing slant, and he began to linger with his touch when he handed me something or returned my towel. He started holding my jewelry for me during practice. After practice was over, he would take my necklace from his pocket, place it around my neck, and fasten it for me. It was difficult to gauge whether these were all elements of a kind man doing what he would do for anyone, or whether he was paying special attention, playing the same game I was. Whatever the case, these moments were the highlights of my days.

One afternoon, Liz and I went to my house after school, to study and gossip. We went straight to my bedroom, which was warm with the early March heat wave, and I cracked the window open. A slight breeze blew through the window to stir the air in the room.

I glanced across the room to make sure that the door was closed, and noticed that the breeze was rustling the Bill Clinton poster I kept above my desk. I ran to the desk to secure the poster. "Close the window, Liz!" I shouted. "Billy's falling down!"

Liz jumped up and slid the window shut. She looked at me as I pressed on the tape at the corners of the poster, and then laughed. "You and your Billy, Izzy," she said. "You're too funny. Isn't it enough that you have that damn black and white portrait of him on your school binder? Do you need to have him everywhere? You don't have anything else on your wall!"

I chuckled as I sat on the swivel chair.

"You know I love Billy," I told her. "You can take anything away from me, but not my Billy." All my friends laughed at my obsession with our nation's president, but they had their Luke Perry and Jason Priestley, and I had my Billy. I loved politics, I loved the fact that President Bush had not been re-elected, and I loved that this relatively young Democrat - a witty and smart silver-haired fox from Arkansas - had won the presidency. My black and white poster of Billy was all I wanted to decorate my bedroom; it was all the inspiration I needed.

Liz and I sat down to talk and before long our conversation turned to her new - and significantly older - boyfriend. I was dying of jealousy, and wanted to know every detail about their relationship. Liz was open enough with me that she didn't mind sharing, and we were in the middle of a very telling story when the door to my bedroom flew open. We both jumped guiltily, and turned to find my dad standing in the doorway, wearing one of his signature low-browed looks. Anyone unfamiliar with my father would have thought that he was angry, and on the verge of a lecture, but Liz was accustomed to my dad's brutish nature. She'd seen his various moods before, and understood as well as I that he wasn't actually distressed or upset. She looked up at him, giving him her most innocent smile.

"Hi, Dad," I said quietly. "What is it?"

Someone was here to see me, he informed me in Spanish, already disappearing down the hallway. He was gone before I could ask who it was. I exchanged perplexed looks with Liz, and we hopped to our feet.

Mr. Stevens was standing at the front door when I got there.

"Hi," he said.

I stared at him, unable to hide my surprise.

"Uh, hi," was all I managed. What was he doing here? How did he know where I lived? I felt a familiar throbbing in my chest; my heart was pounding as I moved forward.

"Can I come in?" Mr. Stevens asked, looking straight at me. I suddenly felt under-dressed, wearing my sweats and an old navy-blue tank top. My hair was dry, but I had allowed it to air-dry after practice and it didn't have any style of its own. I put my hand to my head self-consciously, thinking that it must look a mess.

"Uh, sure, of course," I replied, taking a step back to let him in.

Mr. Stevens stepped into the living room, taking in the big screen TV, the set of olive green Italian leather couches, the issues of *Architectural Digest* stacked neatly on the oak coffee table. From the expression on his face, I could tell that he was surprised to see such expensive furniture and fittings inside a house in my immigrant neighborhood.

Our terrier had darted from her cushion on the floor to greet the stranger, and he bent down to pat her. She pulled one of her favorite tricks and turned on her back to show him her belly.

"What an adorable little thing you are," he said, rubbing her smooth belly affectionately.

"She's a terrier mix," I said, just to fill the void. "She was my fifteenth birthday present."

Mr. Stevens straightened and looked at me again, while Brownie continued to sniff his Birkenstocks. He nodded, but didn't answer.

I paused then plunged forward. "Uh, can I help you with something, Mr. Stevens?" I asked nervously. I had gone through the entire day in my head, but couldn't find any reason for this surprise visit.

He nodded suddenly, as if he'd just remembered. "Of course, how rude of me. You forgot your necklace and your watch at practice." He reached into his pocket to pull them out. "I brought them for you. I didn't want you to be worried."

He held his hand out, the silver necklace and pendant dangling from his fingers, and I realized that this was the first time that I had forgotten about my jewelry. I stared at the necklace and blinked a couple of times, feeling bad that I hadn't even missed them until now, when Mr. Stevens was standing in my living room holding them in his hand.

"I completely forgot about them," I confessed. "Thanks so much for going out of your way to drop them off."

"It's no trouble," he replied. "I gave a few swimmers a ride home and one of them told me that you lived right down the road so I thought, why not? It's on my way. I didn't want you to panic thinking you had lost them."

As he spoke, he gently pressed the jewelry into my hand, lightly caressing my wrist as he released them. We locked eyes for a moment and I felt the instant heat of an all-too-familiar blush appear on my face. He must have noticed it too, because he looked away and added, "At least now you can rest well knowing that your grandmother's necklace is safely back with you."

I frowned in confusion then remembered that I had told him that it was my grandmother's necklace the first time I asked him to hold it for me. "Yes, I'm glad to have it back," I answered quickly. "It's really sweet of you to drop these off. I really appreciate it."

We walked to the door, and Mr. Stevens stepped out to the porch. He looked back at me before he walked away, paused, and then winked and said goodnight. I walked back inside, still stunned, my grandmother's necklace clutched in my hand, and closed the door behind me. I was promptly pounced on by a very excited Liz, who had apparently been eavesdropping on my conversation with Mr. Stevens from the hallway.

"Oh my God! I can't believe it! Izzy, he is so into you!" she gushed. "Oh my God. Can't you see? He drove out of his way to give you the jewelry, when he could have just given it to you tomorrow at school. Don't you get it? He wanted to see you, that's why he came to your house!" She bounced up and down, fizzing with excitement, and my lips turned up in a smile. I couldn't believe that he had come to my house, and I certainly wasn't going to guess at his intentions, but maybe she was right. Had he come all this way – even made up an excuse to do so – just to see me again, outside of school?

Was this the start of more meetings? Could I dare to hope for something like that?

Before I could reply, my dad appeared again, standing in front of us in the hallway. I wasn't concerned about whether he'd overheard Liz squealing or understood what she'd said -- he did not speak or understand English well, despite having lived in California for over ten years. He didn't need to speak English for work, and had stubbornly refused to adapt to his new homeland's culture, despite my mother's pleas. He didn't know what Liz had said, or what had passed between Mr. Stevens and me. His face was stern as he asked to speak to me in private, though, and I wondered what he thought. Liz glanced at me and quickly scurried off to my bedroom.

When Liz was gone, my father asked bluntly who that man was. I explained that he was my swim coach from school, and that he had stopped by to drop off the jewelry that I had forgotten at practice.

My father didn't seem moved by the explanation.

"I don't like him," he told me in Spanish, his tone deadly serious. "I don't want you spending time alone with him. Do you understand me?"

My mouth dropped open in surprise. I couldn't believe that my father would pass judgment on Mr. Stevens so hastily, and with so little reason. He hadn't even been introduced to the man, and this was one of my coaches! I began to defend Mr. Stevens, telling my father that he this was my swim coach, that he was a good man, and that he'd just given other swimmers a ride home from practice. Why was my father being so unreasonable?

"I know what I'm talking about," was my father's sharp reply. "Be careful, Isabel."

I paused, trying to decide what to do; in my family, an order from my father was law, and it was difficult to get around it. My father took my silence for agreement and turned away. I stood where I was and watched him go, my heart and mind racing.

Chapter Four

Sowing the Seeds of Love

By the middle of the term, I was surreptitiously stalking Mr. Stevens. I arrived at school early each morning to sneak a peek into his classroom. If he was there, and the door was open, I sat across the hall, pretending to read, and watched him through my lashes. If he wasn't, I went to another area of the school, where everyone would have to pass me to enter. If I hadn't seen him by first or second period, I did everything I could think of to track him throughout the lunch period. Sometimes I saw him standing outside his classroom, looking my way as I walked toward my faded brown locker between periods. Sometimes I saw him standing in the hallway across from the locker itself. Sometimes I even saw him standing outside one of my classrooms.

I began to think that he was tracking my whereabouts as well.

I fell behind in my studies, because I spent most of class time daydreaming, creating lengthy and vivid scenarios where Mr. Stevens' desire for me was so intense that he was willing to risk everything – including his career and his marriage – to be with me.

These scenarios became progressively more intense, and signified a progression in my imaginary relationship. Today, I knew that I would find my way into a deeper and more taboo sort of daydream. Several days earlier, I had dreamt that Mr. Stevens finally confessed his attraction to me. On the next day my fantasy involved him whisking me off my feet in a deep, passionate kiss. Today, I knew, would be no different. I hadn't seen him since arriving at school, and it was now third period. I was missing him terribly, and couldn't wait to sit down and start thinking about what we would be doing if we were together. I spent most of Algebra II class fantasizing about what might come after the kiss. Would he decide that he could no longer live without me?

After third period, I made my way to my locker alone. Liz and I had third period together, and she usually walked with me to our fourth-period class, but she was out sick today. I walked quickly toward my locker to begin the age-old process of dropping off one book and picking up another, and ducked down to fish a new pen out of the case at the bottom of the locker.

As I straightened, I realized that someone was watching me. I stilled, throwing my senses out, and realized that someone was standing right *behind* me. I smiled to myself; I recognized the smell of his cologne, a clean and masculine scent, and didn't even need to turn around to know who was there.

I turned, my eyes cast down so that I could feign surprise when I saw him. Mr. Stevens was standing closer to me than he had ever stood before, leaning toward me as though he was about to speak. I breathed out, trying to keep my cool, and looked up at him.

"Are you looking for me, Mr. Stevens?" I asked coyly.

He looked at me for a moment, then leaned forward and reached into my open locker to thumb through my books. I turned to stare at his hand as he poked through my neatly organized set of schoolbooks, utterly confused.

"I'm looking for my letter," he replied quietly, so that only I could hear. His breath was warm against my neck, his chest nearly touching my back, and my heart began to race. What was he talking about? A letter? What letter? I didn't keep any letters in my locker. Did he think that I had stolen something from him?

"What letter?" I finally asked, feeling somewhat unnerved. "I was under the impression that my locker contained *my* belongings--"

As soon as those words escaped my mouth, I realized exactly what Mr. Stevens was trying to say. He wanted a letter *from* me! He expected that I had written a letter to him, and he was looking for it in my locker.

There was no letter, of course, but he was telling me what he wanted. He was *asking* me to write him a letter.

I felt a warm flush on my cheeks and raised my hands to them, seeking to rub away the blush that would give me away. Looking across the hall, I noticed one of the boys from my English class looking at us, and looked down again. When I looked up at Mr. Stevens, he was smiling down at me. He must have seen my confusion, because he chuckled slightly and drew back, gazing down at me with those beautiful hazel eyes. He had thick, dark eyelashes that framed his eyes, and drew them down now to look at my feet. Fireworks were going off in my stomach, and I didn't know how much longer I could stand there.

"Sure," I heard myself saying, "I can do that."

Mr. Stevens smiled and reached out to touch my bare shoulder in thanks, then stepped back. As he turned and walked toward his classroom, he looked back at me and said, meaningfully, "I'll be expecting it soon." before disappearing into his classroom.

I gasped and watched him walk away, trying to regain my senses. I had no memory of any conversation taking place. What had I just agreed to? And how much trouble was it going to cause?

Halfway through fourth period, I remembered exactly what I had agreed to. I was sitting in class, staring out the window, still trying to recover from the intensity of my physical reaction to him, when the whispered phrase echoed through my mind. It came in Mr. Stevens' low voice, whispered against my ear. "Write me a letter," he had murmured quietly. And I had told him that I would.

My mind flew through the possibilities. Maybe I was reading too much into it, maybe he was teasing me because he knew that I had a crush on him, maybe he was trying to get me in trouble. But maybe, my heart said, maybe ... he was interested in me the way I was interested in him. Maybe he just wanted to hear me say that I was interested.

I couldn't believe that my fantasy was merging with reality. The very idea was completely overwhelming, and I didn't know if I could deal with the repercussions. He was onto me. He knew exactly what I was feeling, and probably what I was thinking, and he was commenting on it. But hadn't that been my intent all along? That thought made me pause and I frowned. Had I really intended for something to happen between Mr. Stevens and me? I had to admit that I'd never thought about that aspect, and I didn't actually know the answer to the question. That alone bothered me; I'd always known exactly what I wanted, and gone after it. The idea that I hadn't known what I wanted in this case ...

My heart continued to race through the end of the day, and I rushed to swim practice to find that everything there was business as usual. The girls were full of their daily jokes and laughter and had no idea that the whole world had changed, at least for me. I slipped into my suit and got in the pool with the other girls to start our daily workout, wondering what the practice would bring.

Nothing different, as it turned out; we went through our standard reps of freestyle, breast stroke, back stroke, and butterfly, with a long warm-down at the end of practice. I looked up at the coaches every time I came to the edge of the pool, but never caught Coach Stevens' eyes on me. Perhaps I had over exaggerated, I thought. Maybe it was all in my head.

By the end of practice, I was too tired to think about anything at all. I finished my last lap and drifted to the edge of the pool, then grabbed the concrete coping and pulled myself out onto the deck. The March sun was warm and inviting, and I laid back, letting my feet dangle in the cool water. The sun was bright and warm above me, drying the drops of water on my skin, and I threw myself backward to rest on the deck and rested my arms over my eyes to shade the sun. The warmth of the concrete seeped into my back and shoulders, relaxing my overworked body. I sighed deeply and allowed my mind to rest, focusing simply on the nice warmth on my body.

Suddenly, though, someone came between the sun and me, casting a shadow across my face and bringing the chill of shade. I moved my arm and cracked one eye, then opened both eyes wide. Mr. Stevens was standing over me, holding my towel. He dropped it over my face, laughing, and turned to talk to Natalie. She returned his small talk, then strolled away toward the locker room. Mr. Stevens and I were alone. This was nothing new; we generally stayed together after practice, talking as we walked toward the locker rooms. Normally, though, I walked to the girl's locker room and he went toward his truck.

Today he reached out to take my hand at the gate.

"Isabel, do you want a ride home?" he asked quietly. "I can drop you off at Liz's house, if you'd like, instead of yours."

That was a good idea, though Mr. Stevens couldn't have known the reason for it. I knew that if my dad saw Mr. Stevens dropping me off at home - especially after his stern warning to me - he would completely freak out. I'd be in for a long lecture about obedience and the importance of safety, and lectures from my father were never pleasant affairs. If Mr. Stevens dropped me of at Liz' house, on the other hand…

"Sure," I said lightly. "Liz will be happy to get a visit, she's home sick today."

"Yeah, I know," he answered wryly. "I figured she was, since she's not here. I haven't seen the two of you separated in weeks. I need to change, but I'll be out in ten minutes - we can meet at my truck." He began to turn around, then paused. "Isabel," he said quietly, "it would probably be best if people didn't see you getting into my truck. Let's keep this between us, okay?"

I nodded wordlessly, wondering what on earth he meant by that.

I got into the locker room and rushed through my usual routine - pulling off my wet and clingy suit, jumping in the shower to wash the smell of chlorine in my hair, and struggling with the challenge of slipping my damp legs into tight leggings. I paused on my way out and sprayed on some of my *Exclamation* over my wrists and on my neck.

I trotted out of the locker room and toward the parking lot, hoping that no one was watching me. Unfortunately, my luck wasn't that good.

"Isabel!" one of the other swim coaches shouted. She came toward me, clutching a piece of paper in her hand. She held it out to me when she arrived, and took a moment to catch her breath. "Your times at the last meet. I wanted to tell you how surprised – and impressed – I was at your performance. You've improved so much over the season, and we're all quite … proud of you." Her voice caught on the last phrase, and I knew that it bothered her to have to say it. The two female coaches had made it clear that they didn't like me from the start, and my fast times were forcing them to do exactly what they didn't want to do – acknowledge my progress.

Normally I would have stayed with her, reveling in this praise, and asking for more of it. There was a dark Isabel, deep inside, that liked to see this particular coach squirm, and I loved to take advantage of situations like this. Today, though, I was in a hurry. I knew that Mr. Stevens was probably already at his truck waiting for me, and felt both anxious and excited about what he would say to me. I mumbled a quick thanks to the coach's blank face, then turned and left her standing there.

Ahead of me, I could see that Mr. Stevens was indeed at his truck, with a group of other students already packed into the back seat. I heaved a sigh of relief and regret; I wouldn't be riding alone with him, then. I knew he'd done this to protect my reputation, and his, but felt slightly disappointed. I was looking forward to getting him alone, though I didn't have a clue what I'd say or do if that were to happen. Instead of an intimate conversation, though, we would have a rowdy, crowded ride. I slid into the front seat and scooted toward him on the bench so that two other students could fit into the seat next to me. This put my knee right up against his, and I gulped. The truck was filled with incessant chatter and laughter, but all I could feel was the gentle pressure of his knee against mine. I could hear only the beating of my own heart.

The other students disappeared one by one, as we drove past houses and through neighborhoods to take them home. The drone of teenage chatter diminished with each drop off, and the air began to fill with a different kind of tension. We finally came to the last house, and the girl who sat to my right – the last swimmer in the truck – opened the door and hopped out.

"Thanks, Coach!" she shouted. She waved at us both and sprinted toward the house, leaving us alone in the truck.

We drove toward Liz' house, and it finally occurred to me that he had zigzagged through town at least three times, taking the most direct route to the houses of the other swimmers, but purposely choosing to drop me off last. I gulped down my excitement and nervousness, and wondered fleetingly if I should move away from Mr. Stevens, toward the other end of the bench seat, next to the passenger window. The truck was empty, and there was no need for me to be sitting so close to him. He seemed to hear my thought, though, and spoke before I could move.

"I'd like it if you just stayed where you are," he murmured quietly, anticipating my move. I swallowed and nodded without answering.

We drove in silence for several long moments. Mr. Stevens appeared to be thinking about something; he wore an intense expression, and focused closely on the road as we drove toward Liz's house. The silence finally became too much for me, and I spoke.

"So," I began, hoping that my nerves didn't show in my voice, "what exactly do you want me to write in this letter you've requested?"

I had half expected to hear a snicker in response, or at the very least a quiet chuckle, but his face grew more serious. At the next light, he stopped and turned toward me. His hazel eyes were gentle but intense in his face, and he pursed his lips before speaking.

"Isabel, I think that there are a lot of things you want to say to me, but maybe you're afraid to say them," he replied simply. "Write what you feel. Just be open and honest with me. Do you think you can do that?"

I wasn't prepared for such raw honesty, and it shocked me. I turned from him to stare straight ahead through the windshield, dumbstruck. That was it? He wanted me to just write down what I felt about him? What did that mean? What would I write? What *could* I write? Surely not the truth!

Realizing that time only stood still in my head, I finally managed a response.

"Yeah," I said quietly. "I think I can handle that. Is that it?"

Mr. Stevens smiled, and I thought I saw a hint of relief in his eyes, as if a heavy weight had been lifted off his shoulders. The tension around his mouth and eyes eased a bit, and his shoulders dropped. The light turned green and we continued on our way without speaking again. When we pulled up next to the curb at Liz's house, I gathered my swim bag and school books. I could feel Mr. Stevens' gaze lingering on my every move, and wondered if he'd say anything else. I slid out of the truck without a word, though, and turned back to wave. Mr. Stevens' eyes locked with mine, and I was taken aback by the intensity and tenderness in his eyes. He hadn't said anything when I left the truck, but his eyes left little doubt in my mind. I had been right the first time – he wanted my letter to say what he felt in his own heart.

This relationship wasn't only playing out in my mind.

I practically pranced to the front door, my heart hammering away in my chest, and rapped smartly on the window pane. Just wait until Liz heard about *this*!

Liz was lying cozily on her bed in her flannel pajamas, despite the heat of the day, recovering from her throat infection. Her face lit up when she saw me walk through her bedroom door. I rushed in without thinking and tripped over a pile of her clothes on the floor in my excitement. Before I knew it, I was bouncing up and down on her bed and making her laugh out loud.

"Doesn't your mom make you clean this place up?" I complained, although I couldn't quite muster annoyance. "You've got crap all over the floor. I can barely make out the color of the carpet!"

"No one's as anally retentive as you are, Isabel," Liz countered with a hoarse voice, "Some of us are normal."

I told her about the events of the day and the ride home, in specific detail, and went on to tell her what I thought the whole day might mean. We spent much of the afternoon talking about the letter I would write to Mr. Stevens and going through the possible formats. I wanted to take a more reserved approach, hinting at my feelings and leaving the door open for Mr. Stevens to respond. I mean, what if his intentions were totally innocent and he just wanted me to share my feelings about school, friends, and teenage difficulties? If I poured out my true feelings and he didn't share them, I would be humiliated. Liz said that she didn't think his intentions were innocent.

"Teachers don't just randomly ask students to write them letters and tell them what they're feeling," she replied quickly. "If you were having problems, then sure. If you were on drugs or skipping out on school or your mom and dad were going through a separation, maybe. But you're a great student and you're on your way to college. Your family life is terrific. What on earth would he want you to write about other than your feelings for *him*?" She paused for a moment, letting that sink in. "You should be completely honest with him," she finally concluded. "The only way you're going to make anything happen is by telling him how you feel."

I listened carefully and reluctantly agreed. Liz was right, after all - if I wanted something to happen, I had to tell him so. He wasn't going to guess it. Knowing that, though, didn't make it any easier.

I spent hours composing the letter later that evening. I had eaten two ham and cheese empanadas at dinner, but they hadn't settled well, and I felt like I was going to throw up. The lingering smell of food in the house wasn't helping, and the constant threat of my father walking into my room and lecturing me had me on edge.

I looked up at my poster of Bill Clinton, and prayed silently for help.

This was the most important letter I had ever written, and I wanted it to be exactly right. It had to explain my feelings without coming off as pushy or immature. It had to show the depth of my emotion without being sappy. Most importantly, it had to sound as though it came from someone serious - I knew enough about Mr. Stevens to know that he would never engage with me if I were immature. I finally found a flow that I liked, and settled - with the assistance of my heavy, hardcover volume of Webster's Dictionary - on language that sounded sophisticated and smart. By the time I folded the letter and put it into an envelope, my hand had cramped up and I was overcome with mental exhaustion. It was done, though, and I knew that I was doing the right thing. I had told him exactly how I felt, and had been completely honest. As of tomorrow, for better or worse, Mr. Stevens would know exactly what was in my heart.

In the morning, I met Liz at our shared locker as usual, and gave her a tired grin. Posters throughout the hall advertised the Junior/Senior Prom, which was coming up in June. The posters were promotional and were intended to encourage us to go, but really just taunted those of us who didn't have dates, I thought.

"Not like I want to go anyhow," I told Liz, pointing to the nearest ruined poster. The spring rains had ruined the paper and caused the ink to run. "Corny, overpriced dance. Knowing this school, it will be in the gym rather than any place interesting."

Liz threw me a confused glance, and frowned. "What's with you this morning?" she asked quietly. "I thought you loved that kind of social thing. An excuse to get dressed up, and all that." She held my eyes, waiting for an answer, and I shrugged.

"I'm tired, and worried," I admitted. "I wrote that letter, and I'm not sure it was the right thing to do. I didn't sleep well."

She grinned and pinched my arm. "You worry too much." She paused and looked past my shoulder and smiled. "Besides,

I don't think you have much to worry about. Looks like some-one's waiting for you."

I turned at her words and scanned the walkway behind me. Mr. Stevens was there, standing casually in his class-room doorway at the other end of the hallway. He was look-ing directly at us, though he seemed to be just gazing into space. I couldn't help but be jealous of his cool appeal. He seemed so comfortable in his skin, so confident. I didn't think that anything could rattle him, and I wondered if he'd ever doubted anything in his entire life. I looked openly at him, assuming that he wasn't actually looking back at me, and gasped when his gaze sharpened on my face. He winked, then grinned and turned away, and I laughed aloud. I walked forward slowly, leaving Liz behind. As I got closer, I realized that his eyes weren't as carefree and confident as I had thought. There was a nervousness to him that I'd never seen before, as though he was waiting for bad news.

"Good morning, Isabel," he said as I halted in front of him. "How are you?"

I gave him a nervous smile in response. "I'm fine, though my hand is a bit cramped from so much writing. And I didn't get much sleep."

Those words seemed to put a smile on his face. He stepped closer and handed me a thick Algebra book. I stared down at it, nervous and baffled, and gave him a questioning look.

Mr. Stevens reached out, opened the heavy book, and whispered, "Just drop the letter in the book so that I can walk away with it."

"Ah," I breathed, understanding. I slipped the letter between the pages and handed the book back to him.

"Thanks," he said. "I look forward to reading it. Now, you'd better get to class, I don't want to be the reason you're late."

I blushed slightly, but nodded and turned. Mr. Stevens gave me a quick smile before he walked toward his classroom at the end of the hall.

For the rest of the morning, my friends spent their time asking me why I was walking around grinning like a fool.

Chapter Five

Sweetest Taboo

The chlorinated water felt especially refreshing on my skin. It was a hot spring day, and I had been flushed with nervous energy all day. The smooth repetitive act of swimming laps lulled me into a state of relaxation, and I focused on counting the number of strokes and alternating right- and left-sided breaths. I felt the secure pressure of my swim cap and looked through my goggles at the water around me, taking in the serene blue scenery. The water was cool and smooth against my legs, and the laps came easily. Since the first day of practice, this space had become my sacred ground, where I was free to think and dream without worrying about anything at all.

49

Today, though, thoughts of Mr. Stevens crept steadily into my mind as I swam. I was sure that he'd read my letter by now, and had come to his own conclusions about its content and my intentions. What had he thought? Did my letter expose too much? Was it too forward? Did I scare him off with my honesty? Why hadn't he arrived at swim practice yet? Why hadn't I sensed him searching for me throughout the day? I had looked for him between periods and even during lunch, but hadn't seen him. I worried about how he may have reacted to the letter, and whether he was now avoiding me, but tried to table my thoughts and focus on swimming. What was done was done, and I couldn't do anything about it now.

I would just have to wait and see what happened.

I swam nearly twenty uninterrupted laps, deep in thought, and came to the wall for one final turn. As I reached for the wall to make my turn, I was surprised to feel a strong hand grab my wrist above the water. The grip jolted me from my thoughts and back into reality, and I gasped. I peered through my foggy swim goggles, trying to figure out who had grabbed me, and realized that it was Mr. Stevens. He hunched over the edge of the pool, his brown leather Birkenstocks at eye-level.

I quickly removed my goggles and glanced around; the other girls were at the opposite end of the pool, listening to the instructions being spouted off by the female coaches. I was alone at this end of the pool with Mr. Stevens.

"Isabel," he loosened his grip slightly but didn't let go. "I just wanted to tell you that I really enjoyed reading your letter." He paused, and his fingers caressed my wet wrist softly; I held my breath. "After practice, let me give you a ride home. Is Liz with you today?"

"Yeah, she's coming by after practice. Can you give us both a ride?"

"Of course." He smiled, then straightened and stepped away. I had to bite my lip to keep my excitement and jubilation in check. I took a deep breath and tried to appear normal. In my head, though, I was repeating the same mantra over and over: he liked my letter, he liked my letter, oh my God, *he liked my letter!*

I began to re-read my letter to Mr. Stevens in my head, refreshing my memory in preparation for his potential reaction.

March 13, 1993

(Not quite sure how to address this letter. Should it be Mr. Stevens? Coach? Tom?-- you decide and let me know later),

I was a bit surprised when you asked me to write you a letter. I didn't know what you expected, but then I realized that you'd said you wanted to know what I was feeling, and if there were things that I wanted to say to you but hadn't yet. Sure, there are many things I want to say to you. And no, I would probably never work up the courage to actually say them. Writing things down is definitely an easier way for me to express myself and be more honest...so thanks for the opportunity. And here it goes.

Once I decided that I was going to write this letter, I wasn't sure how to go about it. I wanted to be prim and proper and superficial in this letter, to be respectful, but what's the point of that? I've decided to be honest instead, though that's just a tiny first step. This is the first time I've done something so ... well, bold, and the truth is that it scares me. You're a teacher more than twice my age, and I know you're married with kids, but I feel extremely attracted to you, and it's getting worse every day.

There, it's said, and no going back now.

This attraction, it seems to come out of nowhere, but it makes me feel happy and safe. There's something about you that's so warm and tender, and I love the way your eyes sparkle when you smile at me, the way you steal sneak peeks at me during the school day. And yes, I've seen you do that.

I realize that I might be way out of line here, but you asked for the truth and I hope you're prepared to deal with it. I'm sure this is not the first time a younger girl has flirted with you, and I would completely understand if you take the contents of this letter as a schoolgirl's crush. I wouldn't think any less of you. But in some weird way, I sense a spark, a connection between us. This is all very new for me, and I've never felt this way about anyone before. I've never thought that anyone else felt this way about me. But my heart skips a beat every time you smile at me. Am I crazy, or do you feel it too? I guess as a teacher, you probably have to be guarded with your feelings, right? You're probably not allowed to tell me what you're feeling, though I wish you would.

You know, I reserve certain smiles for you, certain glances, and certain laughs … my best expressions, all saved just for you. In the last few weeks, I've noticed that you've gone out of your way to find me during the school day and speak to me at practice, and I think you might be saving your best smiles for me too. I'm sure you've noticed that I sit very close to you in the truck when you drive us home, even when I'm the only one left in the truck and there's space to spare. And I can't stop thinking about how it would feel to have your lips meet mine.

Well, there it is. I don't know if you'll agree or if you'll make fun of me for this, but you asked for a letter. You asked for honesty, and here it is; totally inappropriate, but honest. I hope that I haven't been too out of line, and that you can still bear to be around me. If nothing is to come of this, so be it. I hope that we can at least continue to be friends.

Hugs (maybe kisses),

Isabel

I had moved on to breaststroke now, and punctuated my breaths with thoughts and silent comments. Who was I kidding? There were thousands of ways he could have taken my letter, though none of them were innocent. The more important thing would be his reaction.

As I came up for air during my last lap of the afternoon, I saw Liz standing with Mr. Stevens near the benches. She was serious as she spoke and was shaking her head. They were both looking my way.

I got out of the swimming pool and dripped my way toward them, my body covered with goose bumps from the evaporating water. I didn't care about the chill, though; I wanted to know what was being said about me. Liz took one look at my chilled arms and beat Mr. Stevens to my swim bag. She threw my towel at me, laughing.

"Here you go sweetie," she joked. "Get that wrapped around you before you catch cold!"

Mr. Stevens gave Liz a pointed look as he came closer to give me my jewelry. I thanked him and continued to hold his gaze while re-fastening the towel around my waist.

"So Mr. Stevens, do you think Isabel looks better dry or wet?" Liz quipped, and my mouth dropped open in shock. I glanced from Liz back to Mr. Stevens, horrified, but saw that he was taking the question in stride, and chuckling.

"Well, I'm not sure," he answered, looking me up and down. "I don't know if I should answer that." A flush of heat engulfed my cheeks and I glared at Liz.

"Well then, I guess we could agree at least that she looks pretty good in a bathing suit, am I right?" Liz grinned at me unapologetically.

To my surprise, Mr. Stevens laughed again. "You got me there, Liz."

Liz nodded, giving me a mischievous grin, and tossed off one last remark as we walked toward the locker room. "All I know is, if I looked that good in a bathing suit, 'I'm sure I would have lots of admirers."

I hit her in the arm to shut her up, then dragged her into the building before she could say anything else.

Ten minutes later, Liz and I were in Mr. Stevens' truck, and on our way to her house. She sat in the back seat with three other swimmers, while I sat in the front, between Mr. Stevens and two other swimmers. As usual, I was pushed up against him, with our legs and arms touching. I felt a sense of closeness to Mr. Stevens that I had never felt before, and not just from sitting so close. I'd sat this close to him before. Today, though, the closeness was emotional. He knew what I felt, and I surmised that he felt the same way. If I concentrated enough, I thought I could probably feel his heart beating through the pulse of his right arm up against my body. I imagined that his heart was beating in rhythm with mine, and smiled to myself.

Mr. Stevens saw my smile and nudged me in the arm. "Something funny?" he murmured quietly.

I shook my head mutely, afraid to speak. I was both terrified and elated at this new emotional connection, and it was almost more than I could handle. The tension of having so many other people in the truck was making it hard for me to breathe, though I didn't think I was ready for them to leave quite yet. I had fantasized about this moment for months. Now that it was here, I didn't know if I was ready. Had I gone too far? Had I started something that I didn't want to finish?

Mr. Stevens dropped the other students off first, as usual, and soon only Liz and I were left in the truck. I glanced at her in the rearview mirror, but she widened her eyes slightly and then looked out the window. She wouldn't be moving to the front seat, then; she was going to leave Mr. Stevens and me alone.

"Mr. Stevens, would you mind turning up the radio?" she asked coyly, watching me in the mirror as she spoke.

He reached across me to turn the radio up slightly, and I grinned. Liz had just given us the cover we needed if we wanted to talk. I glanced down at my legs, and realized that they were almost completely bear next to his. His hand was resting on his own leg, mere centimeters from mine. His hand moved slowly to the slight space between us, coming just short of touching my bare leg, and stopped. I gazed at his hand for a moment, considering, and realized that this was a silent question. He was asking my permission to touch me.

I reached down and took his hand in mind, pulling it gently into my lap. His hand tightened involuntarily on my own and I gulped. I had been touched by guys before, I had been kissed, and I had been embraced, but this was altogether different. This innocent act of holding hands was something more than I'd ever felt. Molten lava rushed through my veins and into my stomach, and it was all I could do to keep from gasping out loud.

Mr. Stevens must have felt it too, since he suddenly grew tense, as if he'd just realized what he was doing, and withdrew his hand. I felt stung at first, but then saw the raw vulnerability on his face. He looked stunned, conflicted, and bewildered in a way that I had never seen before. He glanced at me and shook his head, giving me a wordless look. *This confuses me too*, it read, and I nodded. He was going through the same things I was, struggling with these feelings, and the fact that we weren't allowed to act on them. He was also married, with kids, and was in a worse position than I was. I suddenly felt sorry for him.

I placed my hand on his again and squeezed it tightly. He looked at me, his eyes wide, with a younger look than I had ever noticed.

"Don't worry," I whispered. "It'll be okay."

Chapter Six

More than Words

My parents hadn't recognized the changes in me during the last few weeks; they were too preoccupied with moving plans and finances. Since immigrating to the United States, they had built a dream of returning to Chile, our country of birth, for good. They were in the U.S. to earn and save money, and to give their kids a chance to be citizens of a larger country, but they themselves wanted to return home. After nearly ten years in the United States, my parents felt they had saved enough money to buy a home and start a business, and the Chilean economy had taken a turn for the better in the last few years.

I had, of course, been told since I was five years old that we were in the U.S. for a limited amount of time. This was only our temporary home, they told me, and we would go back to Chile one day. Because of this, nothing in my American life had ever seemed permanent. I viewed all of my pursuits as temporary. My fascination with Mr. Stevens fell squarely into this category: short-term entertainment. I believed that we would be leaving the United States before the beginning of my junior year, so the next few months were my playground.

Everything changed at the end of March. The day should have ended the same way every other day did: a trip to the pool, a leisurely swim practice, some casual flirting with Mr. Stevens, and a ride to Liz's house.

I went to practice as normal, and swam my standard work-out. After my shower, I went to sit on the concrete benches at the far end of the pool area to wait for Liz. Instead of my friend, though, I found Mr. Stevens walking toward me. He was wearing fitted khaki shorts and a white polo shirt that revealed his perfectly shaped and tanned arms, but I refused to look up and notice him. My swim goggles had smudges on the lenses, and I was rubbing them firmly to clean them before taking a comfortable seat on the bench. Suddenly, Mr. Stevens was standing close behind me with my necklace in his hands, and whispering against my neck.

"Isabel, lift your hair so I can fasten this."

Chills rose on my flesh and I shivered in response.

"What's wrong?" he asked, his voice low. "Are you cold?"

"Yes," I mumbled. "My suit is still damp." I looked around, trying to appear casual. Other swimmers had started to talk about us, near the entrance of the metal gate that separated the pool from the track and field, and I knew how this scene would look if anyone saw us. A married adult teacher, standing closely behind a fifteen-year old female student, leaving little room for anything but a breeze to pass between their two bodies.

"Well I'll hurry then," he answered, draping my necklace around my neck and pulling it back to fasten it. I remained perfectly still while a torrent of fluttering butterflies flew about in my stomach, while his fingers lightly caressed the nape of my neck.

"Why don't you meet me in my classroom in ten minutes," Mr. Stevens murmured, stepping back. I closed my eyes against the rush of emotion, and turned my head back to look at him. His face was unreadable - perfectly masculine profile, straight nose, and a carefully groomed light brown goatee, a bit darker than his dirty blonde hair, which framed his lips so nicely. His eyes were lighter than usual, almost a shade of green and the way they gazed at me took my breath away.

"Okay," I whispered. "I'll meet you there."

"I'll be waiting, Isabel."

The distance between the locker room and Mr. Stevens' classroom, roughly a quarter of a mile, felt like one of the longest walks I had ever taken. My mind was clouded with fear, excitement, and anticipation. Thoughts chased each other through my brain with each step; what did Mr. Stevens expect of me? What if he wanted to kiss me? What about my braces and the rubber bands that the dentist required me to wear daily? How would I keep my composure? What if I just turned around and headed straight home, only two blocks in the other direction? With every question came doubt, and with more doubt came anxiety.

By the time I made it to Mr. Stevens' classroom, I felt overwhelmed and worried. The door was closed, and my attempt to turn the thick, metal doorknob failed. I formed a fist with my right hand and knocked lightly on the door, just once. *If the door doesn't open in the next ten seconds*, I thought, *I'll walk away as quickly as possible and pretend that this never happened. I won't think about it again.*

As I was getting ready to walk away, though, the doorknob clicked and turned. The door opened slightly with a slow creak. My heart jumped and I took a deep breath. Mr. Stevens' face appeared in the narrow space between the door and the doorway, and his eyes scanned the open space behind me.

"Quickly," he said. "Come in."

I slipped through the door and Mr. Stevens pulled it shut behind me, ushering me toward the center of the room. I put my bag down on a school desk and stood there, not knowing what to expect, but he motioned me forward, taking my hand and pulling me toward him gently into his embrace.

"We should stay away from the windows," he whispered into my hair, "but we can do what we want in here. No one can see us standing here."

The comfortable embrace lingered for what seemed to be minutes. Mr. Stevens' hands explored my body, first tracing the planes of my back and arms, then focusing on my waist, taking the time to feel under my fitted black cotton tank top. I held tightly to his body, running my hands up and down his back and enjoying the warm feel of the fabric of his polo shirt. I didn't know if his body tingled as intensely as mine, but I could feel his heart pounding against my chest and knew he could likely feel mine as well. We stood there, locked in a tender embrace, for an eternity it seemed. I didn't want it to end.

"Isabel," Mr. Stevens whispered in my ear. "I never thought we would get to this point."

I felt his grip loosen just enough to create a slender gap between our two bodies. He pulled back slightly and his cheek brushed up against mine, I could feel the five o'clock shadow on his face. We moved toward each other and I shifted my face slightly, finding his lips with my own. I had kissed boys before and knew how it was supposed to feel, but was shocked at the lightning that struck when our lips met for the very first time.

Our lips met time and time again, first slowly and gently, and then more urgently and passionately. Our hands explored the uncharted territory of each other's bodies, and our movements grew frenzied. Mr. Stevens placed one of his hands soothingly on the nape of my neck and guided me as he kissed me more deeply. I had no idea how much time had passed before we finally pulled apart, both breathless and flushed. Mr. Stevens let out a soft chuckle and stroked my hair.

"Now, I'm sure you've had some practice at this," he said, "because you're such a good kisser."

"I've had some practice," I replied with a sly smile, "but it's never been as good as this."

He smiled, one of those big smiles that exposed his white teeth and made his bright hazel eyes sparkle with delight.

"You know, if I didn't already know you had braces, I would've never known you wear them from the way you kiss," he told me.

I'd worn braces for the past twelve months, and had learned to be very careful while kissing, to make sure that my braces never got in the way. I couldn't resist asking, though. "Haven't you ever kissed a girl with braces before?"

An incredulous and hurt look clouded his face. "Isabel, do you think I'm in the habit of kissing schoolgirls? Do you think that's why you're here?"

The tone of his voice was defensive, but there was something else behind his question. I realized he didn't want me to think he was messing around with me. He didn't want me to think that what we were engaging in was something flippant or commonplace.

"That's not what I meant," I answered quickly, trying to reassure him. "I was just curious, that's all. What am I supposed to think? You're here kissing me, so why would it be so crazy for me to think that maybe you've kissed a schoolgirl or two before this?"

Mr. Stevens abruptly loosened his grip on me and stepped back.

"Isabel, I need you to understand that I've never done anything like this before," he said, looking straight into my eyes, his tone serious. "In answer to your question, yes, I've kissed someone with braces before … when I was sixteen. And no, I don't go around kissing schoolgirls. I've been a teacher for over ten years and this has never happened before, and-"

I put a hand up to his lips, stopping him. "That's not what I think," I said softly. "I wouldn't be here if I thought you were like that. I was attracted to you from the first day we met, and I didn't even know you were married then. I was just curious if you had ever been with someone else as young as me, that's all. I didn't mean to imply that this is what you do for kicks."

Mr. Stevens relaxed a little; I could see it in his body language. He placed his right hand on my left cheek, and then leaned forward and embraced me again, as carefully as if he were dealing with a priceless porcelain doll.

"You understand what I'm risking here, don't you?" he murmured in my ear. "This choice I've made to give in, to hold you, to kiss you…" he pulled back and looked into my eyes. "I'm risking my career, I'm risking my family. I'm risking everything. I could go to jail if I were to get caught, do you know that? I would never do something like this if I didn't sincerely care about you, Isabel. You're not a game to me."

My heart skipped a beat at his words. This had never been anything more to me than a crush, and some kind of conquest. I wanted to break some rules and see how far I could go with Mr.

Stevens, how far I could get him to go. But there were serious repercussions on his end, and it wasn't just a game. Now that I was in his arms, I knew that it was more than a game for me as well; I had developed stronger feelings for him than I realized. It was as if that embrace and that lingering and passionate kiss awakened a love I hadn't felt before, and overwhelming emotion that was new and unexpected. The thought of him going to jail put me into a cold sweat and it was clear that I cared a great deal about this man who was putting his life at risk for me. All of a sudden, I realized that this was an immense responsibility for me, to engage physically with him like this, and to care for the faith he so willingly had in me.

"I know, I really do," I replied. "I believe that you care about me, and it means the world to me. I want you to know that." I took a deep breath and seized the opportunity I'd been waiting for. "Will you write me a letter? So that I know how you honestly feel about me?"

Mr. Stevens seemed to hesitate, but finally he nodded.

"All right," he said, "But you have to be really careful. We both have to be very careful. And after you read the letter you have to destroy it, or give it back to me so that it doesn't end up in the wrong hands."

"You can trust me," I reassured him, "I wouldn't do anything to get you in trouble. But, I don't think I'll want to give it back."

He paused, then nodded again. "I felt the same way about yours," he said, leaning toward me again.

We stole another lingering kiss before I left his classroom. I walked quickly down the hallway, wondering if I looked any different now than I had when I walked into his classroom just an hour before. I felt different. I felt ... alive. I glanced at Principal Warren's office as I walked by, and remembered what Mr. Stevens had said about his life and his career. One of the walls of the Principal's office was glass from floor to ceiling, with mini-blinds obscuring the interior. Was he in there? Was he watching through the glass? Had he seen me leave? What if he knew how long I had been in Mr. Stevens' classroom?

I pushed these thoughts out of my mind and hurried toward the parking lot.

Chapter Seven

Friday, I'm in Love

As time went on, the spring days got longer and stretched toward summer. Sunsets lingered and came later and later in the evening, and the air-dried and warmed toward the hottest months. My afternoons became longer, due to the extended daylight hours, and I was thankful for that, because it allowed me to maximize my time with Mr. Stevens in his classroom after school, where I spent three to four afternoons every week.

At least once a week, though, our swim team traveled to a meet at another high school. We never hosted the meets at our school, as our practice pool was too small. The additional travel made the afternoons even longer, and tortured me endlessly. I ached to be near Mr. Stevens in every sense, and being around him in such a public place was sheer torture. Seeing him across the swimming pool, keeping time on the races and keeping official scores ... it pained me to be so far from him, but the last thing I wanted to do was expose him. He had risked so much to touch me, kiss me, hold me, and care for me, and I didn't want to ruin that or endanger our relationship. The knowledge that we were breaking the law was exciting, but also a bit frightening, and I didn't want either of us to get caught. So I bit my lip and controlled my feelings, and tried to seem distant and aloof around him when we were in public.

"What's up with you?" Vicky asked one day during practice. "Did Mr. Stevens piss you off or something?"

"No, nothing's wrong. He didn't piss me off. Why?" I asked, suspicious of her motives. Had she seen something? Did she know what was going on? "What makes you think I'm pissed off at him? Did someone say something?"

Vicky shrugged. "No. But you used to hang out with him all the time, and now you avoid him like the plague. Whenever he comes over to talk to us, you walk away. What's all that about?"

I realized suddenly that I had gone from one extreme to the other in a few weeks. That was a mistake, and people were bound to notice. I couldn't backtrack now, though – the damage was done. What was I supposed to say? *"Yeah, I'm staying away from Mr. Stevens because I don't want anyone to know I'm making out with him after practice"* would never do.

"You know, he was pretty cool at first," I replied as non-chalantly as possible. "But one day I was late for practice and he made me go to the diving pool to swim laps. I'm not going to hang around with him if he's going to be such a jerk, you know?"

That answer must have been good enough for Vicky, because she lightly tapped my shoulder and then jumped into the water to swim off. I laughed as I watched her swim away; she was doing the butterfly - badly - and bumping into other swimmers as she shimmied from side to side down the crowded lane. My smile faded, though, when I realized that she was probably voicing what everyone else had noticed as well. My sudden change of attitude had been just that - sudden and unexpected - and people were going to wonder why. I had to come up with a better story, and quick, or change my behavior again and hope that no one else said anything.

I wasn't sure which option was best, or which would cause me more pain. Our late- afternoon rendezvous were becom-ing more and more intense, and my senses were becoming fragile. When I walked toward his classroom, now, I knew that there would be more physical contact, with less clothing. We hadn't gone all the way yet, and Mr. Stevens was always very careful about my feelings - he asked me if I was okay with what we were doing every five minutes, it seemed - but we were both getting braver, and closer. I didn't know if I could be close to him without really wanting him, but I was afraid of getting hurt.

I didn't realize it at the time, but I was also starting to fall in love with him.

He had asked me to call him Tom after a couple secret meetings, and nothing delighted me more. It gave me a sense of belonging and intimacy – a secret that we shared together, rather than a secret I shared only with a teacher. He had started writing me letters, and I adored them. I blushed, smiled, giggled, and sighed with content when reading about his feelings, desires and emotions.

Today was one of the days when I had to head straight home from school – to maintain some appearances, Tom said – and my heart was heavy at the thought of going home without seeing him. I found a letter in my locker, though, which improved my mood. I rushed down the two blocks between the school and my house, ran through the door and into the house, shouted a quick hello to my mother in the kitchen, and rushed to my bedroom.

"Isabel, are you okay?" she shouted after me, her voice worried. She had asked me the same question several times, and I wondered how much she knew. I thought that she had probably noticed my extended absences and preoccupation. I was sure that she'd noticed my obsession with being at swim practice every afternoon. She'd also made comments about the fact that I'd begun to wear more fitted clothing and wear makeup to school, something I had never done before. She hadn't asked me why, though, and I didn't plan to tell her.

This particular secret wasn't ready for sharing, quite yet. Given the nature of the secret, I told myself, I didn't know if I would *ever* share it.

"I'm fine, Mami," I shouted down the hallway. "Just have homework that needs to get done." I waited for a moment to see if she was going to respond, then closed the door to the outside world and jumped on my bed. I got cozy under the fluffy comforter, then pulled the letter out of its envelope.

Dear Isabel,

I read your letters over and over again before I destroy them – and even then, that's the last thing I want to do. I don't have a choice, though. I wish I could keep them, and reread them whenever I want. Your words ease my mind and bring a joy that I have not felt in years. But I'm terrified that they'll be discovered.

I've never felt totally comfortable writing to you, because I'm very concerned that someone will find the letters and use them against me. But I know we both express our feelings much more honestly on paper than face to face, and I want you to know what's in my heart when the words coming from my mouth fail me. As long as you destroy the letters I write to you, or return them to me, I have no reason to worry.

I wanted to tell you, Isabel, that you're doing great. You do such a great job ignoring me when we're in public that it almost hurts, though I know that it's necessary. I'm not as good at it – sometimes I'm foolish and I get too close to you when we're at school or at the pool, and I should know better. I know that you're protecting me, sometimes much more than I protect myself ... and for this, I'm very grateful.

You've turned my life upside down, Isabel, and I don't mean that in a bad way at all. I know it wasn't your intention, or mine, to end up in this kind of relationship. I'm not the most poetic or romantic guy in the world, but I can tell you this: my heart skips a beat when I see you walk by; my heart races when you glance my way and smile; and the way you look at me, that look that you save just for me, it makes me forget to breathe. I've never been the jealous type, but it bothers me so much when I see guys looking at you, or even coming by the pool to flirt with you. That's the kind of power you have over me, Isabel. I don't think you even realize it!

I can't wait to hold you in my arms again and kiss your perfect soft lips.

Thinking of you,

Tom

I sighed and held the letter to my chest. Although Tom expected me to destroy each letter he wrote me after I read it, I strayed from the protocol. How could I possibly destroy such priceless letters, coldly rip his precious words to shreds without having anything to show for it? He may not want a record of our relationship, but I wanted something to keep. I wanted something to look back on years from now, or even next week, when I needed a happy thought. My mind was a sponge but it could never absorb every detail, every sweet word he wrote to me.

I rose from my bed and checked the hallway. Empty. I listened closely, and heard my mom banging away in the kitchen, cooking up whatever we were having for dinner. My brother was in the living room watching TV. That meant that I had at least ten minutes to myself. I moved out of my room and snuck down the hall to my mom's office, which sat right across from my parents' bedroom. This was the tricky part; I had to make it into her office without being seen by anyone in the house, or they would ask me what I was doing. And I was doing something I wasn't supposed to be doing - making a photocopy of the newest letter from Tom. I had copies of each handwritten note, letter, and card he'd sent me, stuffed neatly into a shoebox in the back of my closet. The originals, of course, went back to Mr. Stevens. I didn't know what he did with them, but I assumed that he destroyed them.

The photocopies - which he didn't know about - were mine to keep.

I usually kept the letters to myself, though I let Liz read them when she was over. She adored them, and always kept me up late into the night asking me about the day's events. Tonight Sarah was spending the night, and I'd decided to share the letters with her as well. I knew that she wouldn't approve, but something in me thought that if she could only read how much he loved me, understand how much I meant to him …

I was very wrong, and her reaction was stunning. She finished the last letter, her face turning redder with each word, and finally threw it down on the ground.

"What the hell? Is he crazy?" she blurted out. "How can he be writing such letters to you? He's married! I can't believe you're becoming all giddy and happy about this! It's wrong!"

"Sarah, keep your voice down!" I shouted in a whisper. "I don't want my whole family knowing about this! And I know this whole thing is wrong, Sarah, I get that!" I looked down at my hands. "I wish Mr. Stevens wasn't married, I wish I were closer to his age, I wish things were different! But they're not. You think it's easy for him? Don't you see how he's struggling with all this? With the decisions he's made?"

"Isabel, I won't ever understand it," Sarah replied quietly. "My dad was one of those guys. He left my mom and ran off with some other woman, did you know that? He was one of those men who made the 'tough decision' to leave us. So please don't try to make me like Mr. Stevens or see where he's coming from, because I don't want to and I don't think I ever will."

I looked at Sarah and, for a long moment, didn't know what to say. I heard what she was saying, but I didn't want to lose her. I could see now that it had been a mistake to share the letters with her, and that I had to find a way to fix it. I finally decided that it was probably best to lie to her.

"Sarah," I said, meeting her gaze, "I'm not a home-wrecker. I know I'm really into it right now, but you know me – these things never keep my attention. I'm not going to go any farther with it. I mean, I'm moving back to Chile anyway, and by the end of the summer I'll be ten thousand miles away from here. Trust me, even if Mr. Stevens got it in his head that he wanted to leave his wife to be with me – which he's never even hinted at, by the way – I would never let him do that to his family." I swallowed, hoping that she believed me. I had tried not to think about the move to Chile, since it would mean an end to my relationship with Tom, but it was a convenient deadline. If it got her off my back, it would make me feel better.

She nodded, but frowned. "Izzy, you're my friend. I don't want to think badly of you. But you should never have told me about this. I think you're playing with fire here, and sooner or later this will all come out in the open and you both will be in big trouble."

The month of May flew by and soon it was the end of swim season, which meant an end to the silly antics and camaraderie of the girls, an end to the outings for the meets, and an end to the early dismissals from class. I was heartbroken. It would also be the end of my daily poolside interaction with Mr. Stevens.

I assumed that I would still get to see him some afternoons, but I would no longer have an easy and believable excuse to see him every day as I had done since March.

A few days before the last swim meet of the season, in the privacy of his classroom, we spoke about the future.

"Isabel, what are we going to do when swim season ends? Are you going to skip out on me?"

I wasn't expecting this question, and he must have seen the perplexed look on my face. I hadn't thought about what we were going to do, and I had certainly never thought of an end to our relationship. I wanted things to continue just as they were, despite what I'd told Sarah.

He must have read the thoughts all over my face. "What? You haven't thought of that? It hasn't crossed your mind, that the end of the season might bring an end to … this?"

I shook my head slowly. "I don't think our relationship revolves around the swimming pool, does it?" I asked. "I spend most of my time trying to ignore you at the pool, so why would swim season define our relationship?"

He looked at me with a new light of admiration in his eyes and stretched his arms toward me. My body had already found its way to his and we held each other in the murky gloom of the darkroom. The smell of the developing chemicals surrounded us; so distasteful to some, but I had learned to associate those strong scents with the man who stood before me. I sunk into our embrace, sighing with satisfaction.

"Promise me that you'll still come around," he whispered suddenly. "Even if it's only a couple of times a week."

"Of course I'll come around," I whispered back. "You know what? We'll probably have more time to spend with each other once swim season is out of the way."

He laughed then held me closer.

With the end of swim season, Tom and I did indeed find more time to spend together. Swim practice had always taken up at least two hours of our time after school, and with practice out of the way, we were free to enjoy these earlier hours together. We met in his classroom the first week, but I was becoming more and more nervous about people around us at school. I thought that they would soon start making the logical connections.

The after-school janitor hours were also unpredictable, and grew dangerous. Tom and I were kissing in the darkroom in his classroom one afternoon when a janitor unlocked the main door of the classroom and walked in. We were out of the janitor's sight, but I jumped with panic and immediately let go of Tom. He put a finger to my lips and shook his head quietly, asking me to keep quiet. We both stilled, hoping that the janitor would just walk out of the classroom and leave us undiscovered. When it became apparent that he wasn't leaving anytime soon, Tom shrugged and stepped out of the darkroom. I remained behind, pressed into one of the corners, and ready to dart under the counter if need be.

"Good afternoon," Tom greeted the janitor, stepping from the darkroom.

"Oh, I'm sorry," the janitor said, surprised. "I didn't think there was anyone around."

"It's all right," Tom assured him. "I sometimes stick around until five or so, working in the darkroom. If you could come by after five in the future, I would really appreciate it. That way I don't get in your way."

I held my breath as the janitor paused, thinking. What if he refused? What if he insisted on cleaning the entire classroom right now? What if he pushed past Tom to enter the darkroom and empty the garbage in here?

Were we about to be exposed by the man who cleaned the premises?

The janitor finally agreed though, and said that he could rearrange his schedule. He apologized once again in his thickly Spanish-accented English, and I heard the sound of the heavy door shutting behind him. I breathed out slowly, trying to still my racing heart, and heard Tom's steps as he entered the dark room again.

His eyes were large and frightened, and his shoulders were tense. "We need to start meeting off-campus," he noted quietly, his voice strained. "This was too close."

I nodded wordlessly then carefully walked out of the dark room with Tom closely behind me. "I'm going to go home, Tom. I don't want to risk being here any longer."

He nodded, and tenderly kissed me goodbye.

The next day, I met Tom in the school parking lot by his truck at three o'clock sharp. We weren't planning on leaving together, since that would be obvious, but we wanted to check in with each other before we left school. It was early summer, and I was wearing the same thing most of the other California girls wore – short shorts and a light, fluttery summer top. I knew that I looked good. My legs were extraordinarily long – I had earned the nickname "Legs" from boys at school – and I never shied away from wearing short shorts or skirts that barely reached mid thigh. I knew that Tom was particularly fond of my legs, and liked it when I showed them off. He was never short on compliments.

I walked quickly toward the entry of the parking lot and turned left; we were planning to meet at a coffee shop several blocks down, where I could sit and do homework while he watched out for people we might know. I quickened my pace when I left school and nearly sprinted to the shop, to get there before he did. I wanted to get a chilled drink and cool down before we left.

Tom arrived in a matter of minutes, though, and took one look around the shop and the parking lot outside. I watched him through my sunglasses and rose when I saw him walk back out to the truck. That was the sign that we were in the clear; no one we knew had entered the shop yet, and the parking lot was empty. I sprinted to his truck, got in, and laid down on the seat until we were several blocks away. We didn't want anyone to see us together in the truck, or near the campus, for obvious reasons.

"You can sit up now," he muttered out of the side of his mouth. "We're well away from anyone who would recognize us."

I sat up with a sigh of relief, and looked around. "Thank goodness this is not a country town," I replied, laughing. "This would be an impossible feat if we couldn't rely on the anonymity a larger city affords us!"

Tom smiled in response and the tension seemed to dissipate from his fit body. Sitting in his truck was a more pleasant experience now; there were no other students to ride along with us, no excuses of being innocently dropped off at home, and less danger of exposing ourselves with a careless word or gesture. I didn't have to look for excuses to sit close to Tom, as we could already touch each other as much as we wanted, so I sat on the other end of the bench seat, buckled in. He motioned for me to move closer to him and I shook my head, yanking on the seat belt across my chest.

"Safety first," I smiled, teasing.

He shrugged in response and smiled back, his eyes relaxed and happy. "Where do you want to go?" he asked casually.

I shrugged. I had never needed a place to go for some privacy before, though I had heard of places to go, where mountain passes offered privacy and a nice view of rolling valleys. Liz's boyfriend took her to these passes regularly, and I always heard the details. But I didn't know the names of the roads – she just told me that they went up into the mountains.

"Well, there are always the mountains," I suggested. "I've never been up there myself, but I've heard that people drive up there for some privacy."

This made him chuckle slightly. "My thoughts exactly. You see that road up there?" He pointed to a dirt road up ahead and headed toward it. "If you make a left at the very end, the road takes you straight into the heart of these mountains. Don't worry, I'll find a place that's so secluded no one will bother us, at least for a few hours."

He turned onto the road and I saw that it wound up in front of us, switchback style, to achieve a higher elevation. After a few jagged turns, Tom found a small fork on the main road and decided to take it. The road he took was unpaved and quite bumpy, but it only made the adventure more exciting. Bright green, leafy tree branches hovered over the road, and soon the truck was hidden from the main road, under the shade of what seemed like dozens of thickly foliaged trees.

The scene was breathtaking: there were nothing but trees and leaves behind us, and the truck was completely hidden by the thick vegetation overhead. To our right I could see a sharp drop, with a view of the city and valleys below us. If I looked carefully enough, I could even make out the winding road we had taken on our way up. It looked like a slithering ant trail from this elevation.

Tom turned off the loud diesel engine. The silence it left was so pure that I thought I could hear the fluttering wings of butterflies among the trees.

"Oh Tom," I sighed happily. "This place is perfect. Why didn't we come here sooner? Why did we take the risk of staying in that classroom when we could have been out here?"

Instead of answering, Tom unbuckled his seat belt and moved toward me, taking me into his arms. The bench seat of the truck was long and wide enough for us to lay down comfortably, and we took advantage of the new horizontal position. As he lay on top of me, the pleasurable feeling of his weight on me sent tingles up and down my body.

We kissed fervently, without restraint, our kisses moist, deep, and intense. I was lost in the moment, lost in Tom, lost in the heat of our touching bodies. Before I knew it, my shorts were on the floor of the truck, as were my panties and bra. Next to my clothing lay Tom's clothes, including his boxer shorts.

I felt his hips moving into mine, his kisses becoming more sensual, and his mouth wandering from my lips to my neck and then lower, lower, oh God, lower. Tom kissed me in places I had never been kissed before.

Liz had recounted lustful stories about the first time Brad had gone down on her, and it had sounded so sensual and pleasurable; yet, I never imagined that a man's lips down there could feel so incredibly good. My body pulsated with sensation, and I could hardly contain myself. I felt an unfamiliar release of warm fluids, and my body exploded in ecstasy for the first time.

Tom made his way back up, kissing my flat belly, making his way up to my breasts, my neck, and then back to my lips again. He kissed me passionately, and as he did so, I could feel his hips thrusting gently into mine. Although I had nearly lost all my senses, I reached out and stopped him when I felt his hardness against me.

"I don't think we should be doing this," I whispered. I didn't mind lying naked with him and kissing for hours, but I wasn't prepared to go all the way. At least not like this, in the cab of a truck, somewhere in the mountains, with only a few hours to spare.

Tom immediately stopped the movement of his body and lay on top of me, gazing into my eyes.

"You're right," he replied, his voice sleepy. "I don't want to make you feel uncomfortable, and I'm sorry if I went too far. Are you okay?"

"Yes," I whispered back. "In fact, I'm *too* comfortable, and that's what frightens me. This is the first time I've been completely naked with someone else, and everything you're doing feels so incredibly good. But I'm just not ready to go all the way. I feel like there'll be a perfect time and a perfect place for that – and this just isn't it. I think we need to be smart about this, too."

Silence. Tom lifted some of his weight off of me, but still continued to gaze into my eyes with such intensity that I had to look away. He placed his hand softly on my cheek and turned my face toward his.

"Isabel, look at me." I allowed his hand to turn my face toward his, and he continued, "Isabel, you're such an amazing girl, you know that? I got carried away and I should've been the one to stop, not you. I know better, of course I know better. But my body seems to lose control when I'm with you, close to you, because you make me feel amazing. If lying naked with me is as comfortable as you'll be, then that's where we'll draw the line.

85

I'm not here for sex; I hope you know that. I want you to feel completely ready, and if I'm the guy you want to lose your virginity to, I'll wait until you feel it's time."

I reached up and hugged him closely, glad he had assumed I was a virgin, which I was.

"Thank you," I whispered in his ear. "Thank you for understanding me."

He embraced me, one of his hands stroking my long, brown hair, while his other hand held onto my waist firmly.

"I've been dying to say this, but I didn't want to frighten you," he whispered, pulling back slightly, so that his eyes could gaze into mine. "But I can't keep it to myself anymore. Isabel, I'm completely … in love with you."

I must have looked as shocked as I felt. It was an unexpected confession - I always thought that if he said this, it would come much later, if at all. I didn't think he'd say it in person. He rarely said things like this out loud, since it was easier to put on paper. What could I say now? I hadn't expected this, and so hadn't come up with a response. Making sure not to lose his gaze, I opened my mouth slowly; if I delayed for long enough, maybe I would figure out how to respond.

"I've never been in love before," I finally confessed, looking into his eyes. "But I know that I would die if anything happened to you. I know that I can't sleep at night because I want to be at your side. I know that seeing you in the morning brightens my day. If that's what love feels like, then I think I'm in love with you, too."

He smiled, a broad, genuine smile that made my heart skip a beat. He shifted away from me and began to reach for his clothes.

"Can I ask you something else?" I blurted out, wanting to stall him a bit.

He looked back at me. "Sure. What is it?"

I looked at him. "When we're alone," I said. "Can I hold your hand? I think it'll make me feel ... closer to you."

He stared at me, and then chuckled, reaching out to kiss me on the forehead.

"Of course you can," he said. "You're my Isabel."

Chapter Eight

Winds of Change

The swim season had come and gone, and with that, so had my sophomore year. I spent the last few weeks of school in mid-June finalizing the details of my trip to Europe with the French club. It was such an exciting thought … Europe! I had never been outside of the American continent, and this was my chance. It also gave me a chance to see the world before we went back to Chile, which was scheduled at some point during my junior year, an event I was already beginning to dread. Fourteen of us were going, including Vicky, my good friend and fellow swimmer. Mrs. Drake, our dreadfully obese and abrasive French teacher, would serve as the chaperone.

My relationship with Tom had lived through the end of the swim season, and somehow intensified, and was now challenged by the summer break. My mind was filled with questions: how would we continue to see each other without school as a meeting point? How could our relationship endure? Would either one of us be willing to take the time out to continue seeing each other, if it meant going out of our way, and potentially exposing ourselves, to do so? What kind of alibi could I use, what could Tom use as an excuse to go out and meet with me?

Most importantly, how would we handle all of this without attracting notice?

To my pleasant surprise, Tom seemed determined to continue spending as much time as possible with me. Just before the school year ended, we met for coffee in a public space. I told everyone that we were meeting to decide whether I had a future as a swimmer. In reality, we were meeting to figure out how to continue our relationship through summer without drawing attention. We were still limited with regard to meeting outside of school, and there was no way we could pass for a legal couple; I felt like a twenty-four year old inside, but I still looked like a teenage girl. Tom, on the other hand, was visibly older; he couldn't pass for someone in his twenties, with the thin lines around his eyes and the gray peppering his dirty-blonde hair and goatee.

After much deliberation, Tom nailed down a plan. "We can continue to meet at school a few times a week, and then we can drive somewhere else for a few hours," he said. "It gets us away from prying eyes, and gives us a chance to talk. What do you think?"

"Don't you think people at school will get suspicious that I'm meeting you on campus and then driving off with you?" I asked.

"Not really," Tom answered. "Since I'm teaching summer school, you can just blend in with my students, maybe coming in right when class ends. It will just look like you're one of my students, hanging out after class. No one from the administration comes on campus during summer school, so it's actually a safer time for us."

"All right, if you say so," I said, "I just don't want to do anything that may bring attention to us. Last month's rumors were bad enough."

Tom looked wary. "What rumors?"

"Apparently, some of the students noticed our after-school routine," I replied, "and although they knew nothing about what was really going on between us, they began to spread rumors about what they thought you and I were doing when we were leaving campus together." Tom looked alarmed, but I quickly reassured him. "Don't worry, I went ahead and took care of those rumors. I said that I was dating a college guy from UCLA and that I was asking you to give me rides to meet him someplace, so my parents wouldn't be suspicious. I told them I knew you would do it because you gave students rides home all the time. So if anyone asks, I'm dating a guy named David who's an accounting major at UCLA. Other than that, you have nothing to worry about."

"Isabel, you're too much," Tom said, laughing. He stilled and gave me a fond smile. "I should be protecting you, not the other way around. You're supposed to be the vulnerable one. Yet, here you are putting your hand in the fire for me."

I squared my shoulders. "Do I look like I need to be protected?" I asked jokingly. "It wasn't even hard – covering this relationship up is becoming second nature to me, at this point."

Tom chuckled then led me out the door of the coffee shop. It was time for our drive up the mountain.

My daytime escapades with Tom took on an extra touch of excitement during the first half of the summer. Although we limited ourselves to two or three outings a week, Tom began calling me at home on the days we were not scheduled to meet. At first, I was worried. What would I tell my parents when he called? What would they think?

When my mom answered the phone one day, I thought that we were done for. Tom must have asked to speak with me anyway, though, as she walked down the hall a few seconds later and handed me the cordless phone.

"Isabel, it's your friend John on the line," she said quickly.

I looked up, surprised, and saw that she was completely disinterested. It was normal for male friends to call me from time to time, and she didn't think that Tom was any different. I took the phone carefully and rose to shut the door behind her, sighing with relief.

After a few weeks, my parents became accustomed to my friend "John" calling, and they never asked me a single question about him. My parents thought I was too young to have boys over to the house, but phone calls were okay with them. He called on days when we didn't see each other, so we had daily contact one way or another. The summer felt magical, with this new love, the impending trip to Europe, and the possibility of more happening between Tom and I.

Parting ways with Tom was more difficult than I thought it would be. Although I was only going to be away in Europe for two weeks, it felt like I was leaving Tom behind for good. We hadn't been apart since our relationship began in March, and I had spoken to or at least seen Tom every single day since our first kiss. Nearly four months had gone by, and his presence in my life was now a constant. How could I possibly make it through two weeks without him? It was a problem I hadn't thought about before. Now it seemed very big.

"God, I'm really going to miss you," Tom said two days before my departure, during one of our routine mid-day trips to our mountain retreat. "I'm so used to seeing you every day, hearing your voice ... life is going to be pretty boring for me for the next two weeks, while you're having a blast in Europe." He paused. "I'm sure some teenage kid will try to get into your pants, Isabel, so just be careful."

I couldn't help but giggle. "Since when have I not been careful? I'm totally into you, and even when we're together

I'm careful. What makes you think I'm going to let other guys get close to me? I'll be far too busy missing you to even notice anyone else."

"Well said. Just what I wanted to hear," Tom said with a smile, although he quickly sobered. He took me into his arms and continued, "Look Isabel, I know I can be laid back and casual about a lot of things, but not about you. You mean the world to me, and if anything were to happen to you, I would be devastated. I just want you to be safe and I don't want anyone to take advantage of you. Promise me you'll be careful, that you'll be safe if you're drinking or out dancing, because there are some bad people out there. Okay?"

I nuzzled closer to his chest and listened to the sound of his heartbeat. The familiar clean scent of his laundry detergent reminded me of the first time I was close enough to smell him, when we were locked in an embrace in his dimly-lit classroom, forgetting about the world and its rules. Things were so different now, so much more established; I didn't want them to change.

I lifted my head to look Tom in the eyes, noting his love struck look. "You don't have to worry. I'm not going to do anything that would screw this up. You know I'm a responsible person and anyway Mrs. Drake already has all kinds of rules established. According to the contract she made us sign, if we break any rules, we fly home early at the expense of our parents. She'll make sure that we're safe. Don't worry. I'll be thinking about you and missing you like crazy the entire time."

Tom tightened his grip around me. "Isabel, I love you with all my heart. I'll be counting the days until you return."

I squirmed with happiness. His endearments were becoming more and more common, and I loved it when he got romantic.

"Ciao ma, I'll call you as soon as we land in Brussels!"

I leaned through the driver's side window and gave my mom a quick kiss on the cheek. She smiled and blew me a kiss, and I waved and watched her drive off into the distance. Then I lugged my heavy suitcase to the curb in front of the student parking lot, where the rest of the students were chatting and waiting to set off. I made my way over to Vicky; her long, brown hair was tied in a messy bun and she looked up at me and grinned, revealing the metal braces that framed her teeth.

"So, we're going to sit together on the plane, right? I already told Mrs. Drake that we're going to share a room, I think she's already set it all up."

"Cool," I replied eagerly. "You know, Mrs. Drake likes you way more than she likes me – if I had asked, she would have turned me down instantly!"

"Did you see who's coming on the trip with us?" Vicky leaned closer to me with a conspiratorial smile. "R. Y. A. N."

I blinked at her. "Ryan?"

"Yeah. Don't you remember, I had a huge crush on him last year? He was a junior on the swim team."

"Vicky, I wasn't on the swim team last year," I reminded her.

Vicky snapped her fingers. "Oh, that's right. And Ryan quit the team this year, so you two haven't really met."

I glanced over at him, noticing his boyish good looks for the first time. "Vicky, he's not my type anyway," I told her. "I've seen him around school. He hangs out with that Goth group, doesn't he?" I looked over at Ryan again, who was sitting on a bench nearby, looking at his passport. "He looks pretty normal now, though. What happened? It's only been one month since we've been out of school, is that all it takes for him to lose his Goth look?"

"Yeah, he's over that phase," Vicky replied. "I suppose it's because he's going off to college, you know? He probably felt he had to lose the rebel look. But he's still cute, Goth or not. He's got a baby face."

"Well, he does seem more mature than most high school guys, I'll give him that," I conceded, watching Ryan carefully put his passport into his backpack and straighten up, looking around. "He's got pretty blue eyes. And a nice nose."

Vicky laughed out loud, "Yeah, and remember, he's not really a high school guy anymore – he's graduated! That means he's getting close to your target age."

The next few hours were spent getting to the airport, checking in, boarding our plane, and getting comfortable in our assigned seats. When the plane had finally taken off and everyone was watching the on-board entertainment, my mind turned to Tom. Although I enjoyed chatting with Vicky,

I wanted a moment of peace and quiet so I could turn my thoughts inward, to the man I yearned to be with.

Here I was, I realized, sitting in this huge 747 jet, flying at thirty thousand feet across the U.S. and eventually across the vast Atlantic Ocean, which would separate Tom and I for the next two weeks. This was a disconcerting thought, and one that saddened me. Each time my ears popped from the increasing altitude, a greater sense of desperation set in. How would I make it two weeks without seeing Tom? What would he be doing while I was away?

Around me, I could hear the quiet titter of laughter from the passengers watching the movie on the main cabin screen. Although we were well into the full summer season, the plane was air conditioned and freezing. I pulled the thin blanket from the overhead compartment and spread it across Vicky and I, then slouched down in the seat to think. The warmth radiating from her body kept me relatively warm, but I was already yearning for a different warmth; the warmth of Tom's familiar, masculine body. Tom would have kept me warm, with his defined arms and strong hands.

Vicky squirmed next to me under the blanket and suddenly nudged my side.

"Hey, I'm going to make my way to the back of the plane to see if I can chat with Ryan for a while." She gave me a wink as she slid past me to get to the aisle. "Maybe I can hook up with him during the trip or something."

I watched her go, and realized that since Tom and I first kissed in his classroom, I had become completely dedicated to him, forsaking all others. A part of me sometimes wondered why I was so loyal to a man who was literally sleeping with another woman. The fact that she was his wife made it even worse. I often spent hours torturing myself with thoughts of the two of them together; although I had never seen her, in pictures or in person, she was ever-present in my mind. Did Tom find it difficult to be with her when he was supposedly in love with me? I wondered what effect it would have on Tom to imagine me with another guy. Would he be as hurt as I felt? Maybe he would finally be able to empathize with what I was going through.

To be fair to Tom, I never shared these doubts or negative emotions with him. He likely did not know or guess that his relationship with his wife bothered me as much as it did, and that I was hurting. I was very cautious about what I wrote in my letters to him; he was in a difficult position, and I didn't want to make it any worse. I had alluded to the jealousy and sadness that were taking hold of me a couple times, but had pulled back before I said too much. To my surprise, he had picked up on my hints and addressed them in a letter. When Vicky left to talk to Ryan, I pulled the photocopy of that letter out and read it for the hundredth time.

June 12, 1993

Dear Isabel,

This letter won't be very long because I'm writing from home, and it's not very safe for me to write. But I noticed something in your previous letter that concerned me. I can sense that you're sad. Our relationship is affecting you, I mean really affecting you, and I don't feel good about that.

I know that this situation we're in is difficult for both of us, and right now, it may feel like you've got the raw end of the deal. Well, that's not entirely true. I'm not saying it's easy for you, because I can see that it isn't. But you must know that I'm not just having my cake and eating it too. I'm miserable. I want to be with you all of the time. You need to know something: my wife is like a roommate to me. It embarrasses me to say it, because I know she loves me the way that I love you, and it's not fair to her. But I only love her like a friend. We aren't affectionate, not the way I am with you.

It's very important to me that you know that.

I'm sure we both sometimes wish that we could be together the right way (I mean, you and I in a relationship that was mutually exclusive), because our lives would be so much less complicated. And if this is becoming too much for you, if you're feeling bad about all of this, if it's too much for you to handle, you need to talk to me about it. Isabel, please be honest with me and always tell me how you're feeling. We can deal with these things together. I'm here, Isabel, I'm always here for you. And I'm completely yours and no one else's.

Love,

Tom

I folded the letter carefully and slipped it back into my bag. He was only mine, he said, but that didn't keep him from going home to his wife at night. For the first time, I wondered what it would be like if he were coming home to me, instead.

Our first day in Brussels was *magnifique!* The city was not as enchanting and world-renowned as Paris, but it was my first taste of the old-world charm of Europe and I loved it.

We already had a list of rules to follow; Mrs. Drake had laid them out before we left the airport in Brussels, and even put them in a contract for both students and parents to sign. There were three that seemed intended to hamper much of our fun:

1. Boys must remain on boy-only floors, while girls remain on girl-only floors (i.e., there shall be no co-mingling in hotel rooms at any time).
2. Boys and girls may mingle in common areas such as hotel lobbies. Hotel hallways of stairways do not apply.
3. No leaving the hotel premises without a chaperone after seven in the evening.

Vicky and I broke rule number three on our very first night in Brussels. We were rooming together, and had spent most of the afternoon checking into the hotel and listening to a repetition of Mrs. Drake's rules. When she was done, Vicky and I were ready for a good meal. The dinner included in our itinerary was not appealing – we were able to eat some of the bland noodles, but the extremely unsavory poached white fish was out of the question.

A little after eight, back in our antique hotel room and sitting cross legged on the floor already in our pajamas, Vicky asked, "Isabel, aren't you hungry? I'm starving."

"Yeah, I'm hungry," I replied. "What do you say we find our way to a McDonald's? There has to be one within a few blocks from here, right? I think our French is decent enough ... say, *Ou est le McDonald's*?" I tried in a terrible French accent.

Vicky laughed. "Okay, I think we'll manage. We can go in our pajamas, right?"

I looked her up and down. She was wearing an oversized cream-colored Snoopy nightgown, which hung on her frame like an oversized T-shirt. I was sporting a classic pajama set, with striped blue pajama pants, an undershirt – which was more of a white sports bra – and a matching button-up pajama top.

"Yeah, I think we look fine," I said. "Let's go before it's too late."

We walked right out of the hotel in our pajamas and ankle-length socks, and onto the street outside. No one stopped us, and once we were outside we slowed to appreciate the view around us. We employed our badly pronounced French with some people in the street, but didn't receive any help. We did receive several odd stares, though. After walking for nearly an hour, we returned to the hotel room, still hungry because there had been no McDonald's sighting after walking what seemed to be dozens of small city blocks, but excited about our jaunt through the city.

After a week on the road, and with eight days left to go, people began to get much cozier with each other. When we were in France, we shared a tour bus with twenty-eight students from a Washington state high school, and things really began to heat up. Interschool romances sprung up left and right. Vicky had given up on Ryan after heavy flirting didn't elicit any response. She was already on her way to finding a new guy to entertain her: Will, a rich kid from Washington whose dad owned a yacht.

"Ryan is really into someone," Vicky told me one night in our hotel room on the French Riviera. "That's why he didn't respond to me. Do you know who he likes?"

"Are you talking about that flashy girl from Washington?" I replied. "The one who plays tennis and speaks fluent French? What's her name … Tanya?"

Vicky rolled her eyes.

"Your head must be in the clouds, Isabel. Hello! Have you been on the same tour of the French countryside as the rest of us? Are you seriously telling me that you don't know? Ryan likes *you*, Isabel."

I stared at her, shocked. Ryan was always spending time with Vicky and me on the trip, but I thought he just felt comfortable with us because we were from the same school. It never occurred to me that he liked me. From the moment we arrived in Paris, the city of love, to this moment with Vicky, my mind and heart had been on a single track, and that track always led to Tom. I'd admired the country, of course, and had taken a great deal of pictures every time we stopped at a new town or city, but I couldn't wait to get back home to Tom.

"Well, aren't you going to say anything?" Vicky demanded.

"I honestly had no clue," I told her. "I hope you're not upset about this – you know that I didn't lead him on, right? I didn't go after him or anything. Please don't think that I was going after the guy you liked."

"I'm not upset, I don't care if Ryan likes you," Vicky replied. "Things are going well with me and Will. And I *know* Ryan likes you because he told me himself. Apparently, he's been too shy to approach you. He doesn't want to wait too long, though, because the trip will be over in a week. So he'll definitely say something to you soon. I think he's just working up the courage."

"I don't know what I'm going to say," I replied. "You know my rule about high school guys." I paused, then smiled mischievously at her. "Although I must admit, Ryan is really cute, especially now that he's lost that Goth look."

She smiled back, hunching her shoulders with excitement. "Well, think about it anyhow. He's really into you, and he's a great catch!" She paused then winked. "And remember, he's not in high school anymore. He's a college guy, the kind of older guy you like!"

After saying goodnight and retiring to our wooden bunk beds, I thought about what Vicky had said. I thought about

Ryan, and how I would react if he shared his feelings with me. Maybe this time I should just allow myself to go with the flow. Since meeting Tom, I'd given up on all other guys, and I wondered if I was selling myself short. I had gone farther with Tom than anyone else, and I had more experience now. He'd earned my trust and I loved him, but maybe I should see what it was like with another guy before I returned home.

Those brief but betraying thoughts began to get the best of me. I'd been loyal to Tom while we were together, and yet he was sleeping with someone else. He was going home to another woman every day. He had both his wife and me, and he seemed to be okay with that. He said that he loved me in a more pure way than he loved his wife, and that he wanted to be with me, but was that the truth? Could I trust him? And even if I did – even if it was the truth – he still went back to her, and where did that leave me? The image of Tom lying in bed, lovingly embraced by his wife, was just too much for me to bear.

Maybe it was time to turn the tables and let Tom feel what I was feeling: embittered by circumstances and increasingly jealous of his wife. Maybe it was time for me to get out there and see what the rest of the male world had to offer. I decided I would let myself go with the flow. If the flow led me to Ryan's arms temporarily, then so be it.

The next day, Ryan confessed his feelings for me, like Vicky had said he would, and I went along with it, as I'd told myself I should do. We started spending a lot of time together, holding hands during outings at historic sites like the battlefield at Waterloo, and sharing a booth at dinners. He even carried me into the warm Mediterranean waters in the city of Nice in Southern France.

The experience couldn't have been more romantic, but I had no genuine feelings for Ryan. He was a way for me to explore my feelings, and nothing else – a test for me to see how it would feel to be with another guy. I was guarded with Ryan, and didn't feel any physical response to his touch. In fact, I didn't even enjoy his kisses.

The first time our lips met we were on the tour bus and in the midst of the beauty of the Swiss Alps; the bus had just entered a deep, dark, and long tunnel that cut across a range of mountains, and Ryan gently took my face into his hands and engulfed my lips into his. I didn't respond immediately, but then I recalled the decision I had made to go with the flow. My lips began to relax and I followed the movement of Ryan's lips. It felt awkward and out of sync, but I went with the flow.

As soon as we reached Geneva, Switzerland's breathtaking and colorful capital, I left the main group of students to find a payphone. I was immensely desperate – my heart ached to hear Tom's voice, to clearly remember his lips, his tenderness, and his touch. I needed to hear him again, as soon as possible. I mentally calculated the time difference and knew that it would be a good time to call him at home – it was Saturday morning and his wife was usually out with their daughters.

I picked up the phone and began to dial. From inside the glass phone booth, I could see our group being guided by a tour leader through Geneva's main park, near the colorful flower canter in the shape of giant clock on the central lawn. I listened to the ringing tone on the other end of the receiver and began to panic. What if he wasn't home? Or worse, what if his wife had stayed home today and picked up the phone?

"Hello?" came Tom's deep voice. I felt a rush of relief.

"Hi," I whispered. "It's me."

There was a beat of silence.

"Isabel? Where are you?" Tom asked. "I thought you weren't supposed to be back for another week. Oh my God, are you home?"

"I'm in Switzerland right now," I replied. "We just arrived this afternoon."

"You're calling me from Switzerland? Are you crazy? How are you paying for this?"

"Don't worry about it, I'm at a payphone and I've got my mom's calling card," I said into the shiny black receiver. "I've only got a few minutes because Mrs. Drake will come looking for me any minute, but I had to call you. Tom, I miss you so much. I just wanted to hear your voice and to tell you that I've been missing you like crazy."

There was a pause, but I could hear the smile in Tom's voice when he spoke. "I miss you too," he answered. "I've been lonely without you. I keep thinking of the good time you must be having in Europe. You know that I always worry about some other guy showing up and sweeping you off your feet. I know it's really none of my business, but I still can't stop thinking about it."

"You've got nothing to worry about," I replied, keeping an eye on Mrs. Drake and my friends. They were still standing by the flower clock. "I just miss you so much, Tom, and I can't wait until I'm back home with you. I have to go, but I'll save some credit and try to call you again in a few days."

"I miss you too, Isabel. Be good, okay? I love you."

"I love you too. Bye for now."

"Bye, Isabel," he said. I heard the final click on the other end of the line and closed my eyes against the tears.

Mrs. Drake was already frowning at me when I stepped out of the phone booth at the edge of the park. I hurried back to join the rest of the students, who were still listening intently to the tour leader talk about the mechanics of the oversized flower clock on the perfectly mowed lawn.

I would have preferred to share my time in Europe with Tom, but I didn't have that opportunity, so I settled in with Ryan for the next few days, to have some innocent fun. We held hands and cuddled from park to park, we strolled through the cobblestone streets in Monaco, enjoying the mid-summer Mediterranean weather. Our last few days in Europe were spent in Northern France, in the coastal city of Normandy, where the gusty winds required us to wear light sweaters during the cloudless evenings.

"So, have you thought about what will happen when we go back home tomorrow?" Ryan asked on our last night in Normandy, right before the sun touched the horizon on its way to setting on the English Channel.

This was exactly where I did not want the conversation to go. I remained silent for a few moments before I finally spoke.

"Well, I'm not sure if I mentioned this, but at the end of August I'm supposed to move back to Chile with my family," I replied slowly. "We don't have any plans to return. So, I really can't get serious with anyone right now because after I get back, I've got only a month left."

"Oh," Ryan said, fiddling with the vintage dog tags around his neck. "I didn't know that you guys were moving back there permanently. I thought maybe it was just a trip or something."

"I'm sorry, I should've told you from the beginning," I said. "But I thought we were just fooling around. I didn't think that any of this would continue back home. My parents don't allow me to have a boyfriend because I'm not even sixteen yet, so there's no way we can keep seeing each other back in California. It just won't work out, Ryan. I'm sorry."

The cold breeze tousled my long hair, filling the silence between us. After a long moment, Ryan looked up from his dog tags and gazed at the setting sun sinking below the horizon.

"Yeah, I guess it's for the best," he said, not looking at me. My heart sank; I hadn't intended on hurting him, and it had honestly never occurred to me that he might want more than just a brief escapade with me on this trip. He was a nice guy, and didn't deserve to have his heart broken simply because I was exploring my feelings. I reached out and took his hand, trying to apologize with my eyes. He smiled at me, but pulled his hand away and shrugged.

We walked back to the hotel with at least three feet of space separating us.

Ryan became distant and guarded after that, which was okay by me. I spent our last morning in France on the sunny beach again, but this time with a new friend named Heather. She was a mousy-haired freshman from our high school, and we'd become friends during the trip. Vicky was splashing in the water with Will, her new boyfriend from Washington.

"Why didn't Ryan want to come to the beach today?" Heather asked. "It's our last day here, doesn't he want to take some pictures together or something?"

I knew that Vicky was out of earshot, and decided to be somewhat honest. "It's kind of complicated. I sort of ended things with him last night and he took it pretty badly."

"You mean, you broke up with Ryan?" Heather looked at me in amazement. "But why? He's such a great catch, and you seem really into each other."

"I guess he was expecting that we would keep dating back home. That can't happen, though, and he's not happy about it." I shrugged. "The truth is that I'm seeing someone at home. I never told Ryan, I just told him that I couldn't date at home because of my parents."

Heather looked confused. "So you mean you cheated on your boyfriend back home?"

"Well, not really," I tried to clarify, "It's not like he's actually my boyfriend. He's an older guy and he's … married. He even has kids. It's really complicated."

Heather was intrigued. "Who's this guy you're seeing? I mean, how old is he?"

"He's in his late twenties," I lied. "I met him at a nightclub. Like I said, it's complicated, but I'm totally into him, so there's not much I can do about that right now."

I reached down, picked up a jagged rock and drew a big heart in the sand. Within the heart I wrote: "Isabel ♥'s Tom."

Heather laughed, and I looked up at her. "You better erase that before Ryan sees it," she teased. "It will make things even worse!"

I smiled. "You're probably right. Before I do, though, can you take a picture of me with it? I want to give him a picture to prove to him that I was thinking of him, even when I was here. We've never been apart for this long."

"Yeah, sure." Heather took the camera from my hand and snapped a few pictures.

I am not altogether certain if the picture ever made it to Tom's hands after my trip to Europe, but I know that my brief fling with Ryan certainly reached his ears.

Chapter Nine

It Ain't Over 'til It's Over

The trip to Europe had been a liberating experience. I had been out on my own - with some other high school students - seeing the world and making some of my own decisions. More importantly, I had experimented a bit with someone else for the first time since Tom and I started seeing each other, and found that I didn't like it. I had always told myself that my relationship with Tom was something that I could let go of anytime I wanted, and I tested that belief with Ryan while in Europe. I had been wrong about being able to let go of it. The experience with Ryan was like running into a brick wall. The only thing it had taught me was that I couldn't shake what I felt for Tom. In my heart and mind, he was *it*.

The first thing I did when I returned home, before unpacking or calling my friends to let them know I was back, was to call Tom. My mom picked me up before she went to work, so I was home alone. It was a Tuesday morning and I knew Tom didn't have any classes that day, so he would be home. I prayed that his wife would be out, but I couldn't be sure.

I dialed the phone with chills running up my spine, as I waited breathlessly. Tom picked up on the second ring.

"Hello," came Tom's voice. My heart jumped.

"Hi stranger," I said, barely able to contain my excitement. "Did you miss me?"

He chuckled. "So you're back, are you? I thought you'd never return. How are you?"

"I'm good. Just got home this morning. I wanted to give you a call to say hi ... I couldn't wait."

There was a pause. "That's it?" Tom asked. "You just wanted to say hi? Don't you want to see me? Or have you forgotten all about me already?"

I could sense the jealousy in his voice, and wondered if I had somehow given myself away. Did he know that I had been sneaking around with someone else during my time in Europe?

"How could I forget all about you?" I asked hesitantly. "Didn't I call you from Switzerland? I missed you like crazy. I couldn't stop thinking about you, you know that."

A beat of silence. I held my breath. I knew there was no way he could have known what went on between Ryan and me, at least not yet. We had only just returned this morning.

It occurred to me now, though, that he was almost bound to hear about Ryan at some point. Everyone had seen us. Someone would talk. I had made a big mistake, I realized, and hadn't even thought the whole thing through.

"What're you doing in an hour?" Tom finally spoke.

"Seeing you," I answered, smiling. The excitement of seeing him after a two-week separation made my heart race. My heart was burdened with love and jealousy, and my body ached to be as physically close to him as humanly possible.

Our reunion was incredibly passionate. The Southern California summer heat was hard to bear up in our mountain retreat, but all I could think of was how much I wanted to feel him inside my body. I wanted it more than anything I had wanted before, but still didn't feel ready. We had come close to making love before, but we had held back. Now I knew that it was time. Tom's body skillfully caressed mine, and although I could feel *him* pulsating, I trusted him enough to know that I did not have to fear penetration. Tom was content with kissing and being close to me. He was unlike other guys, who were merely interested in "going all the way." He never demanded anything physically of me, and I never felt any pressure from him at all. I had not been ready to give myself up completely yet, but we could lie completely naked without me worrying about what he would do.

"Isabel, I really missed you," Tom said; he was lying gently on top of me, keeping his weight off of me and propping himself up slightly with his elbows. "I care about you so much, and you've changed my life. I don't know what I'm going to do when you leave. We've got about a month left, and then that's it. You're going to move back to Chile, go to a new school, make new friends and fall in love again." He stared into my eyes. "But I'm the one staying behind without you. I'm left here alone."

This is not where I had wanted any of this to go. I had ventured too far, and now Tom's feelings, and my own, were at stake.

"Don't think about those things," I told him, running my nails softly up and down his back, caressing his skin. "Not right now. You don't know what will happen. Maybe you'll meet someone else, or fall back in love with your wife. Maybe you'll forget about me quicker than you think. You never know." These were lies, I realized, and made light of a situation that was far more meaningful for the both of us. I hoped that my trivial comments would ease his heart, though, and make him feel better.

Instead, he took them to heart. He sat up and reached for his clothes, which were scattered on the floor of the truck. He got dressed without looking at me or speaking, and I realized that I had hurt his feelings. I began putting on my clothes as well, and when he reached out to turn the key in the ignition, I stretched out my hand and touched his.

"I didn't mean to upset you, Tom," I said, looking at him. "I was just trying to make you feel better. I don't like to see you like this, and when I do, I feel like it's all my fault because I got us into this."

Tom's expression softened; with his free hand he reached over to caress my cheek.

"Isabel, nothing's your fault," he told me. "You didn't get us into this alone. It takes two to tango, and I don't want you to ever feel guilty about any of this. I'm a sentimental guy, that's just the way I am. Even if you break my heart in the end, I wouldn't regret a single moment of this." He paused, and then continued. "What bothers me is that you think I'll just go out and find someone else to replace you. I don't think you realize that you're more than a fling to me. There was no one before you and there won't be anyone after you. So when I feel sad about you going back to Chile, it's because I'm losing the love of my life."

I took Tom in my arms and embraced him, burying my face in his chest and breathing deeply to take in his scent.

"I'm sorry," I whispered softly, "I know you love me. The fact that you're married makes me insecure, and I'm not used to feeling that way. But I love you. I don't want you to be hurt." I paused and took a deep breath. "Maybe we should look at our relationship as a journey. It may be interrupted here and there, but hopefully we'll keep going. Even after I go back to

Chile, you'll still be in my heart, Tom. And the future may have more in store for us. You never know."

Most of our stuff was shipped back to Santiago by sea, and went weeks before we actually departed from California. We kept only what we needed, and made sure that it could all fit into our suitcases.

"Yes, yes, yes," I muttered into the phone. Liz was making me promise – again – that I would write her at least one letter a week. "Of course I'll be writing you, Liz. What would I do without you? I'm going to count on your advice about all my new friends!" I listened to her laugh on the other end of the line, and smiled. "Listen, Liz, I have to go," I finally told her. "I'll call you tonight, okay?"

I would miss Liz terribly, but I had other things on my mind.

Tom had asked to see me today, and I needed to get out of the house. This was an important meeting. Tom had planned a two-week camping trip with his wife and two young daughters. When Tom first mentioned the camping trip, it hit me like a ton of bricks. It was one thing to know he was married with children, but it was entirely different to hear him making plans to go on holiday with his family. *I* wanted to be the one that Tom went camping with, and I didn't want to think about him enjoying his time with his wife and children.

I walked into his classroom to find it empty. He wasn't waiting for me as he usually did, and I wondered at the difference. I also wondered if he was even going to show up. After a few minutes of waiting, though, he strolled out of the darkroom. He was dressed casually in his khaki shorts and light blue Quicksilver T-shirt. He seemed indifferent when he saw me there.

"Have you been here long?" he asked nonchalantly.

I frowned, wondering what he was doing. "I got here a few minutes ago. You seem pretty busy. Do you want me to let you get back to work? I'm sure you've got a lot of things to get done before your camping trip, right?"

The fine lines around his eyes became more visible, and he barked with forced laughter.

"Yeah, Isabel, I've been busy lately, but not with work or my vacation. I've been busy convincing one of my summer school students that I'm not the guy you're having an affair with. What did you tell Heather, exactly? She came up to me after class yesterday and asked if you and I were together."

"What?" My heart skipped a beat. "Why would she say that?"

"She said that while the two of you were in Europe, you told her that you were going out with a married guy named Tom who had two kids. I'm sure it wasn't difficult for her to put two and two together."

My heart sank as I remembered the conversation. I had been elated at the time, because I was going to see Tom again soon, and I'd been too brave. I had made a huge mistake. I had been too careless with my words to Heather, and should never have revealed Tom's name. My thoughts flew back to that trip, and I wondered nervously what else Heather had told Tom.

"I said that I was dating a guy who was married," I told him, trying to keep my voice even, although there was a mildly hysterical edge to it. "But I never said he was a teacher. I told her it was some guy I met at a nightclub. What did you tell her?"

Tom sat down on the chair across from me and looked me square in the eyes.

"I'm not that worried about Heather because I can see she's just trying to play games," he said. Then his voice hardened. "But tell me something, Isabel. Did you enjoy swapping spit with Ryan?"

I stared at him, dumbfounded, and then looked away, fixing my eyes on the dark stain on the gray-carpeted floor. My cheeks burned with shame.

"You know what? It's not even my business." Tom got to his feet. "You're free to do whatever you like with whomever you like. I have to say, though, that when Heather told me about you and Ryan, I was stunned. I'm sure she *did* put two and two together, not from what you said to her, but from the look on my face. The thought of you kissing him, and doing God knows what else…" Tom broke off and shook his head, a mix of anger and frustration on his face as he glared at me.

From nowhere a surge of confidence rushed through me. If this was to be the end, I thought, so be it. He would know exactly what had happened, and why. I wasn't going to go down without a fight. I looked at Tom, meeting his hurt hazel eyes straight on.

"So now you feel one-tenth of the jealousy I feel," I shot back. "And you're upset and you don't like it. Well, welcome

118

to my world! Do you think I like the thought of you and your wife camping together? Or going to the movies together? Or lying in bed together? I don't like any of those thoughts, but I deal with them without ever trying to make you feel guilty!" I was surprised at the assertiveness in my voice as I surged on. "The fact is, I have to give myself the opportunity to have normal relationships with guys my age. In case you've forgotten, *you're* the married one here! *I'm* the one who gets to go on living by myself!"

There was a terse pause.

"Isabel, I've always been very honest with you, and I don't hide anything from you," Tom finally said, his tone more controlled. "But you don't do the same. You're very reserved with your thoughts and feelings, and most of the time you're that way for my own good. I appreciate that. But I wish you were honest enough to tell me that you made out with Ryan because you felt you had to ... to see what a normal teenage relationship was like. I wish I hadn't had to hear all about it from Heather. You have no idea what a difficult situation that was for me."

"Look, it's not something I *wanted* to do," I argued. "It's something that just happened. And the truth is that kissing Ryan only reminded me of how much I missed and loved you."

Tom walked over to where I stood. He carefully reached for my hand, and then, with nothing but tenderness, he embraced me. He cradled my face in his hands, his eyes staring into mine.

"You know, as much as I love you and am hurt by this revelation…you're my sweetheart, Isabel," he told me. "I don't ever want to hurt you. Let's learn to just be honest with each other from now on, whether it's good or bad. Okay?"

I nodded in agreement as Tom's lips met mine and we made up with a lingering and tender kiss.

Tom's camping trip seemed to affect me much more than my two weeks in Europe had, as far as our time apart was concerned. This time he was the one that was away, and I was the one left behind. To make things worse, I had no way of communicating with him. Apparently it was impossible for him to escape for a few minutes to make a phone call. He was on a family vacation, and I wasn't a part of his family.

I tortured myself by imagining Tom playing with his young girls at a leafy green campground, his wife preparing breakfast over the campfire. During the day they would swim in the lakes and streams and hike through the forest together; at night Tom and his wife would put their children to bed and lie together under the star-filled sky. Tom would make love to his wife, and when it was over, she would rest her head comfortably on his chest.

Would he be thinking of me? Would he think of me when he made love to his wife? Would he wish it were me instead of her? If he was thinking of me, surely he would have found a way to call. After waiting and hoping for a phone call from Tom for a week, though, the painful answer was very clear: not a chance. He had forgotten about me, and was spending time with his family instead.

"I just can't believe it," I raged to Liz as we sat in her back yard under the shade of a large oak tree. "I mean, all he ever talks about is how much he loves me, how much he thinks about me, and how much he needs me. Come on! At least now I know where we stand. Actually, I know where he stands. He's just having some fun with me and that's it. If he really loved me and missed me, he would find a way to call, right? I called him from half way around the world in Europe just to say hello and tell him that I missed him. My mom nearly killed me when she got the bill for that call! She demanded to know who I had called. I thought I was totally busted because she was even going to call the phone company to find out who that number belonged to. I had to lie and say that I had called you to tell you how the trip was going. I took a risk for him, you know? I called because I really missed him. What are you smiling about, Liz? Do you find this funny?"

Liz exhaled as if that was the only way she could shake the smile from her face.

"Oh Izzy, why don't you just forget about him, then?" she asked, as if it were the most straightforward thing in the world for me to do. "This is just too much drama. You're a pretty little thing, and he's a married man. To be honest, I worried about whether he was going to hurt you like this in the end, but I didn't realize that you'd fallen for him the way you have. Why don't you just find someone else to mess around with? I know you think you're in love with him, but it's probably just because he's the first guy you've ever gotten so far with."

I twirled my white rubber flip-flops with the tip of my toe, pondering over her words.

"At least you didn't have sex with him, otherwise you would be feeling pretty lousy right now," Liz continued. "It's hard to tell what his deal is, but in his defense, at least he didn't use you for sex. And you're leaving in three weeks, so he's probably just distancing himself to make it easier, you know? Look, you need to do what's best for *you*. And that shouldn't include sitting here feeling all miserable during your last few weeks in the country. Stop thinking about him. He's made his choice, and you're clearly not it."

"I know. I don't think I can deal with this anymore," I confessed. "I thought I loved him, but let's be honest. I shouldn't be sitting around thinking about what a grown man is doing with his wife, and how that affects me. He doesn't seem to care about me, or that I've only got a few weeks left."

"If I were you, Isabel, I would just enjoy myself with my friends and have a good time before I go back for good. He's just going to ruin your last few weeks here. Do you want to be sad when you leave? Do you want it to be a tragic thing? It's not like you can keep a relationship going from all the way in Chile. He's married, and more than twice your age. You just have to let it go."

Liz was right. I had been thinking the same thing, and she was just confirming it; it was time to forget all about Tom and focus on leaving the United States and starting a new life in

Chile. He had hurt me with his lecture about Ryan and me, he had tried to make me feel guilty for messing around with Ryan when I got home from Europe, and now his silence was clear – he was choosing to think about his family and himself rather than me. It was time for me to do the same.

A few days after my epiphany, Tom returned home and made his first of many attempts to contact me. His efforts were futile; I had made up my mind while he was gone, and I wasn't turning back now. I stopped answering the phone at home and let the answering machine pick up, knowing full well that he would never leave a message. I told my family that if "John" called, I was either not home or busy. My dad naturally welcomed this, although he had no clue who John was. My mom, on the other hand, questioned me.

"Why will you not take this boy's phone calls, Isabel?"

"Mami, don't worry about it," I said, leaning against the kitchen table to watch her prepare her famous *empanadas*. "I just don't want to talk to him, that's all. I've told him, but he's clearly obsessed."

My mom glanced at me through her frameless glasses. She shrugged and continued to stuff the dough disks with a ground beef filling, but she wasn't finished with me.

"Isabel, you shouldn't treat people this way. It's not proper. In fact, it's very rude. If you don't want to talk to him and you want him to stop calling, you should just be honest and tell him that. It's not nice to lead boys on. You wouldn't like it if someone didn't take your calls, would you? You don't have to answer that."

If only my sweet, kind mother had known she was defending an adulterous man more than twice my age. She would have killed him rather than defending him. Then, of course, she would have killed me.

"Fine. Once we leave, I won't ask you to lie to anyone who calls for me," I promised. The *empanadas* would be ready for the oven soon, so I set four of our ivy-trimmed dishes on the kitchen table and placed napkins next to each plate. "But for now, just tell him I'm not home. He's bothering me and I really don't want to talk to him. Okay?"

Tom called my house every day during the last three weeks I was in the country. I felt guilty about ending our relationship so abruptly, and wondered if I should at least tell him what had happened. But my feelings of guilt turned quickly to anger and resentment. Tom was probably only calling because he wanted one last 'go' with me. He knew that I was leaving, so maybe he wanted to get one last kiss or frolic in, I convinced myself. His camping trip and inability to contact me during those two weeks hurt me so much, that I became determined never to see him again.

Saying goodbye to my friends was difficult; yet, it was more of *bon voyage* than *goodbye*. My parents had promised Tony and me that we could come back to the United States once a year on vacation, so I knew I would be seeing my friends again in the not-too-distant future. However, Tony was devastated because he had to leave his girlfriend Amy behind, and although I was trying to perceive the move as a positive event, I was reserving my true feelings for the sake of my parents.

I looked back one more time as we drove away from our house. It was a house I had come to know and love over the years – the one single level, the bright yellow paint, even the massive maple tree in the back. I would miss that, and my life here. My mind drifted to Tom for the last time, and my vision became blurred with tears that seemed to spring from a very deep place in my heart. Had I done the right thing? Would he miss me? Maybe after some time in Chile, I thought, I would write to him and apologize for abruptly ending the one relationship I cherished most.

Chapter Ten

No More "I Love You's"

The southern hemisphere spring was blooming with wild September flowers and thick green foliage when we arrived in Santiago, since the seasons were opposite than what had been my Northern Hemisphere home for so long. My dad, who had traveled back to Chile a month earlier to take care of all the arrangements, was waiting for us at the airport with what appeared to be our entire extended family. The rest of the day was a blur of distantly familiar faces from my childhood: aunts, uncles, cousins, family friends, neighbors, grandparents, and even our former nanny.

Our new house was in a quaint little suburb in Santiago. In Chile, there was no such thing as a mortgage, like there was in the United States; a person had to save for years, even an entire lifetime, to purchase a house in a single cash payment. This was what drove my parents to immigrate to the United States in the first place. They wanted to own a home of their own in Santiago; a home that they could one day leave to their children, as was the Chilean custom. They had spent years struggling and sacrificing in the U.S. to save money for the house. Now that they had accomplished their dreams, we were back.

I fell in love with the house on the first day. Although our house back in California was large and comfortable, it was one of those single-story family homes with bedrooms branching off from a long, straight corridor. This house had two stories, and all the charm of a multi-level home.

"Our first two-story house," I sighed, looking around in appreciation with Tony at my side. I turned to the stairs and started to climb. "Can you imagine how much we would have loved stairs as kids?"

Tony laughed, following me up. "We would have pushed each other down the stairs and killed ourselves before we reached adulthood! I'm just glad we have larger rooms now."

"And more privacy," I agreed. We walked quickly to the end of the hall, where our rooms sat side by side. "And views!" I shouted, running to the window in my room. The vista below me held house upon house, scattered haphazardly through the valley and up over the mountain. Every house was a different shade, with a complementary roof, and trees dotted the land in between. The effect was a startling array of color and nature, and I was beginning to feel some hope about our move back to our motherland.

"If I know you, you'll spend more time with your nose in a book than looking out that window," Tony teased. He was closer than I had noticed and I jumped finding him at the doorway of my new room. I would have to watch that, I thought – I wasn't used to his room being so close to mine, and I'd have to be on the lookout for him sneaking around.

For today, though, we were friends. We were both relatively excited to be back in Chile and to see our extended family once again.

That excitement didn't last long, though. A couple of days after we moved in, my dad asked to meet with us about school. We sat down at the kitchen table, and he pushed a stack of papers my way.

"The school year is over here," he told us in Spanish. "And most of the kids will be out of school for several months on summer vacation. That doesn't mean that you get a six-month summer vacation. The school system in Chile is more rigorous than that in the United States. Based on your transcripts, the public schools will keep you both back at least two years. Tony, you may be kept back three years because the school system here in Chile doesn't recognize U.S. high school diplomas. So you have a choice. You can both get tutors and spend the next few months studying to pass the equivalency exams in time for the new school year, or we can find a reasonably priced

British or American international school that would accept you at your current grade levels."

My heart dropped and Tony whined beside me. What a harsh blow. I would be the most disadvantaged student in school because I attended U.S. public schools my entire life! Another hurdle was our level of Spanish proficiency. Tony had a major advantage over me because he had gone to school in Chile up until the third grade, so he had actually learned how to read and write Spanish. I was only five years old when we left Chile; the only Spanish reading and writing skills were acquired at my elementary school in California, and from speaking with my parents.

"I'm not interested in earning another high school diploma here," Tony replied flatly. "I graduated in the United States. I already have a diploma there, and if they don't accept it here, that's their problem. I'm not going to bust my butt studying for something I already earned in another country."

"That's not an option, Tony," my dad said matter-of-factly. "If you don't revalidate your diploma, you won't get into a Chilean university and you'll have no future."

Tony rolled his eyes and shrugged. "Then I won't go to university here," he countered. "I'll just go back to California where they recognize my high school diploma, get a job, and work my way through college there. I'm eighteen. I can legally do what I want."

My dad jumped up, enraged.

"You think that just because you have a girlfriend there, you can do anything you want?" he shouted at Tony, startling my brother and me. I pulled back, frowning. My dad appeared stoic and angry much of the time, but rarely shouted. "I would like to see you go back to that country and struggle like your mother and I did! You don't have what it takes to make it, you are still a boy! Go if you want, go try to prove yourself. Go show off to your girlfriend! But your mother and I have worked hard to bring you back to a real home, to give you a proper education. If you leave now, don't think you'll be welcomed back!"

Weeks passed, and the spring months gave way to bright and sunny summer skies. Tony and I stayed indoors most of the time; the only people we knew were our cousins and their friends, and we didn't know them very well. It was hard to make friends when we weren't in school, so we spent time with each other, complaining about our fate.

"So we're decided, then," Tony said one day. "We're not going to do what dad wants. We're not going to study for those equivalency exams."

I nodded, frowning at my notebook. I'd been writing a letter to Liz, but nothing had happened during my time in Chile to even write about, so I was struggling. "I agree," I said quietly. "What's the point? There's no way we'll catch up, and even if we pass the exams, we might get into the classes to find that we can't pass them." I paused. We had gone over the scenario again and again, and still hadn't come up with a plausible solution. "I just hate the fact that we worked so hard in school in the U.S, and all for nothing."

"I hate the fact that dad expects us to give up so much, just because he and mom want to live here instead of the U.S.," Tony muttered. He was no longer on speaking terms with my dad, and it made for a somewhat awkward home environment. I was still speaking to my dad, but because it was clear that I was on Tony's side, my dad would often ignore me when I greeted him throughout the day.

As he had promised to do, Tony wrote to his girlfriend almost every day. She was now in her senior year at Royal Oaks. They talked every week, and I knew that Tony had promised to return to the U.S. and marry her. They had some kind of plan, but he wouldn't tell me because he thought that I might reveal it to our parents.

I, on the other hand, spent a lot of my time watching CNN on the big screen TV in the living room downstairs. CNN was my only connection to the United States, and I took full advantage of the twenty-four-hour coverage.

Tony got off the phone one day and came downstairs to join me in the living room. He wouldn't have come in if my dad was there, but it was the middle of the day and I was alone.

"CNN again, eh?" he commented. "Are you thinking of becoming a political consultant or something? International affairs? A war correspondent?"

I shrugged, not in the mood for jokes. "It reminds me of the U.S., and the US feels more like home than this place. The more I watch, the more I remember, and the more I miss it."

"You don't like it here," he said quietly. He didn't give the phrase a question mark, and I knew that he wasn't asking.

We'd been through this several times, and he already knew the answer.

"I thought I would be happy here," I admitted for the tenth time. "I thought we would get here and everything would fall into place. I don't have friends here, though, and I miss my friends at home. I love our house, but dad isn't speaking to you and barely speaks to me. Mom is stuck in the middle of this stand off between dad and us. No one knows where - or if - we're going to school next year." I stopped and thought about the situation for a moment, but still didn't see a way through. "No, I don't like it here," I finished simply. "But what am I supposed to do about it? It's not like I can just leave."

Tony nodded, but didn't say anything. I knew that he had a plan to get home, though I didn't know the extent of it. If he went, though…

"Tony," I said quietly, deciding to take a chance. "When you go back, I hope you'll take me with you."

He looked at me for a moment, but didn't answer. His mouth turned up in a grin, though, and I knew that if he could take me with him, he would.

On a rainy day in October, after moping in the house for months on end and trying to find something to occupy my mind, I finally gave in. I picked up my writing pad and made my way downstairs to the sofa, pen in hand.

I had written so many letters to Tom in the past, but it had been at least four months since I last put my thoughts and feelings on paper for him. I didn't feel the freedom or comfort level I once shared with him, and I wasn't even sure what I would say. But I had bottled up all of my emotions since arriving in Santiago, and I knew that it wasn't healthy. It was time for me to let the emotions out and either bid my final farewell or beg for forgiveness for shutting him out of my life.

October 18, 1993

Dear Tom,

You may never read this letter, but if you do, there are many things that I need you to know. I acted like a coward. I'm fully aware of that. You always treated me with respect, and I was incapable of doing the same. I allowed my jealousy to get the best of me, and while you were away I convinced myself that you were my enemy rather than my lover.

The reason I shut you out of my life so abruptly was because you never called me when you were away on your camping trip. My imagination got away from me, and I thought that it meant that you didn't really love me. I convinced myself that our relationship had been a game to you, and that you'd experienced a newfound love for your wife.

I've had a few months to think about it now, and I under-stand that you probably did miss me. I probably shouldn't have expected you to call me with your wife and kids around. I get that. The truth is, I think I stopped taking your calls because I couldn't face saying goodbye. At the time, it was the only way I could deal with having to let you go. If I were angry enough, then I wouldn't miss you. I lost my mind dur-ing the last few weeks in California, and somehow I took it out on you.

My time in Chile has been more difficult than I ever imagined. It feels like my family is breaking apart. My brother doesn't speak to my dad. My dad keeps me at arm's length, and my mom is caught in the middle. This move has been hard for everyone, but I've been keeping my head up, or at least trying. I've been spending too much time sleep-ing and less time eating. Things are complicated and I don't really want to talk about them now. I miss being able to turn to you with these things, though. I miss feeling comforted by you.

There isn't a day, even with thousands of miles between us, that I don't think of you. You have no idea how much I wish I could be in your arms right now. I've missed your tenderness so much. I dream about you almost every night. I know I've caused you a lot of pain, and I hope you can forgive me. If I could take it all back, I would. That's all I really want to say.

I don't know if our paths will ever cross again, but if they don't, just know that you will always hold a very special place in my heart. I love you.

Tons of kisses,

Isabel

Chapter Eleven

I'll Stand by You

I had walked the four blocks to the small, brick building that housed the local post office many times to mail letters to friends in California. I sent Liz a letter every week, and received the same number in return, with pictures and cards and even gifts from other friends from Royal Oaks. I knew the post office well, and always looked forward to my trips there, as they brought pieces of home to me. But I never found the courage to send the letter I wrote to Tom. I knew that I couldn't send it to his home address, since his wife as likely to find it and even read it. That was far too risky. I had sent post cards to the school when I was in Europe, addressed to Mr. Stevens, and he had received them without any problem. I could have mailed the letter to Royal Oaks and taken my chances.

Something stopped me, though, and the letter to Tom sat in my top drawer, sealed, addressed, and stamped. Waiting.

I wrote my other friends obsessively, and looked forward to their replies. These were the only bright spots in my life in Chile. Mentally, I was keeping track of the U.S. school year -at the end of November, midterms would be coming up, so everyone would be studying and preparing right now. After midterms came and went, we would be enjoying the laid-back days leading up to Thanksgiving, and then it was the Christmas holiday.

It was a shock to realize that I had already lost out on the first semester of my junior year in high school. The worst part was that I didn't know what was going to happen. For all I knew, my dad would refuse to send us to private school and insist on public school instead. If that happened, I might very well end up losing an entire year of school. The move to Chile had taken away the three things I treasured most in life: school, friends, and, of course, Tom.

On an unusually dreary November day, I was rudely awakened from a mid-afternoon nap by the incessant ringing of the phone. My brother was spending the weekend at a tennis camp and Amy knew he was there, so it couldn't be her.

The ringing became louder and louder, and I finally found the strength to get up and drag myself over to the phone in my parents' bedroom. The bed was made, and the room was in perfect order, as usual. I sat on the firm mattress and picked up the heavy receiver of the antique telephone.

"Hola?" I asked in my American-accented Spanish.

"Hi. Is Isabel home? This is Liz calling." I heard what she said, but couldn't understand it. Liz? Since I'd arrived in Chile, none of my friends had called. It was far too expensive to call. We had promised each other that we would only call during emergencies or when we had something important to share. I closed my mouth and cleared the lump from my throat.

"Liz, it's me!" I replied.

"Izzy! I didn't recognize your voice. You sounded just like your mom."

"Yeah, lots of people say that, that's why I've stopped picking up the phone when she's not home. Anyway, what's going on? Did something happen? Did you and Brad finally … you know?"

I could sense some hesitation in Liz's voice. There was as an awkward silence before she finally spoke.

"I've got to tell you something, Isabel," she said, her tone serious. "I really didn't want to have to do this, but I think you should know what's happening here."

Oh my God, Liz was going to drop some kind of bomb and in my depressive state, I wasn't sure I could handle it.

"What is it, Liz?" I demanded. "What's going on?"

"Look I'm just going to say it, okay?" Liz cleared her throat. "The secret's out. Everyone knows about you and Mr. Stevens.

He's been taken in by the police for questioning. The police are here at the school - they took me out of class on Friday and asked me a bunch of questions about you and Mr. Stevens-"

"Liz, you didn't tell them anything, did you?" I cut in, my heart pounding. "Please tell me you backed me up and told them that none of it is true?"

"Izzy, you know that I would be the last person to sell you out like that. I didn't tell them anything. I told them that you guys were friends because he was your swim coach, that's all." She paused. "But they know *everything*, Isabel. The letters you wrote to him, your make-out sessions up in the mountains … everything! They wanted to know if I could corroborate … is that the word they used? I don't remember. They wanted to get testimony from students and teachers at the school, and they were hard-asses, Isabel. Like, they wouldn't let things go …"

I gasped. "How did this happen? How did the police know about Tom and me?" My heart raced and a metallic taste flooded my mouth - the forerunner of the adrenaline coursing through my body. "I've never said anything to anyone about Tom and me. The only friends I ever told were you and Sarah. How did this happen?"

"The police said that Sarah had written a letter to Mrs. Drake, exposing in detail everything you and Mr. Stevens had done," Liz replied slowly. "Sarah wrote that she always told you not to get involved with Mr. Stevens, but that you did it anyway. She said she was disgusted by some of the letters Mr. Stevens wrote to you, and that's why she wanted the authorities to know about what had gone on between you two. The cops didn't let me see the letter, but they kept waving it around and saying that it was all in there, and they didn't seem to believe what I was telling them. They each had a copy of Sarah's letter and I could see that things had been blacked out with a marker, like names or something."

I felt as if someone had sunk a knife into my back. Someone I completely trusted had betrayed me. I realized now why Sarah hadn't replied to any of the letters I'd sent her, and why she hadn't even sent me a birthday card. This must be the reason - she betrayed me and didn't want to tell me about it.

"Oh God," I breathed quietly. Sarah had known everything. I'd told her everything that went on, and even let her read the letters. How could I have been so stupid? Tom had made me promise to keep everything a secret, and I'd gone and given it all away, just to tell one of my friends interesting stories!

That wasn't fair, I reminded myself. I had been telling Sarah the stories to try to prove to her that Tom wasn't a bad guy, that we weren't doing anything wrong, that we were truly in love. That didn't make it any better, I realized now; it had still been a violation of trust, and a huge betrayal.

And now Tom was paying the price for my stupidity.

"Izzy, are you still there?" Liz asked.

"What am I going to do?" I whispered. My chest hurt so much that I could barely breathe. "What about Tom, is he okay? Is he still at school? What have they done with him?

They can't do anything unless they have real proof, right? They need me to admit to something, don't they?"

"That's the other thing, Isabel," Liz said. "Principal Warren asked me for your phone number in Chile. He said that the police wanted to talk to you. I told him that I didn't know if I had it, and he answered that they would just find another way to get it. I thought the best thing would be for you to clear this up yourself, so I gave it to them. But I wanted to call you first to give you some warning so you wouldn't be blindsided by the whole thing. I'm so sorry, Isabel. I hope you're not pissed off at me."

"No, of course I'm not mad at you," I told her, my heart sinking. I suddenly felt exhausted, utterly drained. "They'd find my number sooner or later, anyway. Sarah promised me that she'd keep this a secret. She promised that she wouldn't judge me. I need you to swear - absolutely swear - that you won't do the same thing she did. Promise me that you'll stick to the story, no matter what? Promise me?"

"Sure, Izzy, I won't change my story," Liz assured me. "I'm not like Sarah. Just keep your story straight with the cops if they call … well, *when* they call. Okay?"

"I will. Thanks, Liz. Talk to you soon … hopefully."

"Yup, talk soon. Bye, Isabel."

My mind was spinning as I hung up the phone. Should I tell my parents? Should I warn them before the police called? Or should I hold off telling them, just in case the police dropped the case and never called? What about Tom? What had they done with him? Had the police arrested him? *Could* the police arrest him? Was he still teaching? Did he tell the truth when questioned? Was he even questioned, or was he just thrown into jail? I had heard about how alleged sexual offenders were treated, and the thought sent a cold shiver up my spine. I couldn't bear to think about Tom suffering like that.

I lived by the phone for the next three days, jumping out of my skin each time it rang. The phone call I was dreading didn't come until a week later, at a very bad time. It was Saturday and we had just finished lunch. My mom was washing the dishes, and my dad sat at the kitchen table. Tony was out of the house, and I was just on my way back to my bedroom. It was early afternoon, but I'd been moping all morning and still wore my pajamas.

I froze when I heard the phone ring. A few minutes went by, and then I heard my mom shout out, "Isabel!"

There was a shrill edge in my mother's usually pleasant voice, and that confirmed my worst fears. I ran back downstairs, my mind racing. This was it, then. What on earth was I going to say? And what could I say to my parents? My mom stood in the kitchen with the phone in her hand, a frown on her face.

"Isabel, there's a police officer from the Hillside Police Department on the line," she said sternly. "He asked my permission to question you about a teacher at Royal Oaks. Please tell him exactly what he needs to know."

My mouth grew dry and sticky and I swallowed, trying to find my voice. I took the receiver from my mom's hand, swallowed one more time, then answered.

"Hello?"

"Good afternoon. Am I speaking to Miss Isabel Cruz?" asked a male voice at the other end of the line.

"Yes, that's me," I said, keeping my eye on my mom. She glanced at me, frowned, and walked back to the sink to resume washing the dishes.

"My name is Officer Jeffrey Gray from the Hillside Police Department. I'm calling about Mr. Thomas Stevens, a teacher at Royal Oaks High School. He is currently under investigation."

I made an attempt to sound surprised. "Really?"

"Yes. He has been suspended until the allegations against him are investigated further. Miss Cruz, have you ever been alone with Mr. Stevens, either in his classroom or anywhere else?"

"Yes, on a few occasions," I replied. "He was my swim coach; I never had him as a teacher, but we were friendly during the swim season," I noticed my dad get up from the table and walk into the living room.

"Has Mr. Stevens ever said anything inappropriate to you? Anything sexual?"

"No, never."

"Did Mr. Stevens ever touch you inappropriately, in a sexual manner?"

"No, officer."

"Did Mr. Stevens ever attempt to kiss you?"

"No, of course not."

"Look, Miss Cruz, serious allegations of sexual misconduct with a minor have been brought against Mr. Stevens. We need you to be completely honest with us so that we can get to the bottom of this. Do you understand?"

"Yes, I understand. Do these allegations include several minors? I mean, why are you calling me?" I asked, trying to sound naïve while attempting to extract more information from him. I was shocked and upset, and worried about Tom, but I was also curious about how many people had come forward. Did the allegations include his misconduct with other girls? Part of me had always wondered.

"I'm not at liberty to talk about the specifics of the case," Officer Gray said. "But I can say that you are one of the students named in the allegations against Mr. Stevens. Have you ever witnessed Mr. Stevens speak to or touch any female student in an inappropriate or sexual manner?"

"No, I haven't."

"Has Mr. Stevens ever taken you outside of the school premises in his vehicle?"

"Yes, Mr. Stevens gave me a few rides home after swim practice. But you should know that Mr. Stevens did that for nearly half the team, after practices and meets. He was always very nice to all of us."

"So you're telling me that nothing physical ever went on between you and Mr. Stevens?"

"No, not at all. Mr. Stevens is a really nice person. He's a little flirty but I would say that he's innocently flirty. Maybe

145

some girls, the ones that made the allegations, took his flirty nature the wrong way."

"Let me make this clear, Miss Cruz. I'm asking whether you and Mr. Stevens ever engaged in a physical relationship, whether it be kissing, touching, or hugging. Please just answer the question."

"No, nothing like that ever happened between us," I answered, steadying my voice. How much did they know? How much trouble was he in? If I was the only student named in the case, and I refused to cooperate…

"All right. If that's the case, thank you for your time."

"Sure, Officer." I listened for the *click* and finally the dial tone, then put the phone back in its cradle.

My mother looked over at me from the kitchen sink.

"So, what did the police officer want? Did you give him the information he needed?"

"Yes, Mami, I answered all his questions," I replied. I walked toward the kitchen to help her dry the dishes, praying that she didn't hear the lie in my voice. I didn't look up at her, knowing that she would recognize the lie in my eyes. "They're making a big deal out of nothing with the teacher who was my swim coach. He's a nice guy, but I guess someone said some bad things about him, you know, things that make him look like a bad person."

This was the most extensive conversation about the incident I would ever have with my mom. She dropped it quickly, as an unpleasant thing that she didn't want to discuss. My dad, on the other hand, was much more concerned about the implications. Later that afternoon, he walked into my room without knocking. I pretended to be asleep because I was in no mood to have a conversation with him, but he reached out and placed his rough hand on my head.

"Isabel, get up," he said to me in Spanish. "I want to talk to you about something."

I sat up warily, "What is it, Papi?"

He looked at me with somber eyes.

"Isabel, I hope you were being very honest with that police officer today," he said. "I'm not sure what he asked you, or what answers he was after, but your mother told me that he wanted to ask you about your swim coach. Wasn't that the man that once came to our house to see you? Did anything happen between you and that man? Did he – did he ever touch you?"

Lying to a faceless voice over the phone was one thing, but lying to my father when he was sitting right in front of me was entirely different. I had no other choice, though. I had to keep my story straight, right until the end. For Tom's sake. That meant telling everyone the same story. Only Tom and Liz could know the truth. I just hoped they were telling the same story that I was.

"No, Papi," I told him, looking into his concerned eyes. "Like I told mom and the police, he's just really nice to everyone, and he's friendly to the girls. Someone must have gotten the wrong idea or jumped to conclusions when they saw him giving us rides, or maybe one of the girls took his flirting too seriously. Maybe she got a crush on him then got hurt when he turned her down. That's all. There was nothing going on between us."

My dad looked down at his weathered hands. He looked up again, the expression on his face drawn, as if he were burdened by a terrible, invisible weight.

"Isabel, you're my daughter and I love you," he said, meeting my gaze. "And I believe you, even if the police don't. But if I were to ever find out that you lied to me about this … it would break my heart."

With that my dad stood up and walked out of my bedroom. I watched him go, wondering what he expected me to do. I knew that he had a different view of the world than I did, but I also knew that I was in love with Tom, and looking for a way to protect him. Would I sacrifice Tom's safety – and my love – for my father's emotions? I knew that I would not – they weren't equal risks, and they had vastly different consequences.

As my father left, though, I wondered whether he would ever understand that. Whether he would ever take the time to listen to my side of the story. In my heart, I believed that he had already made his judgment, and judged both Tom and I guilty. I hoped that the police never talked to him about our case.

Chapter Twelve

Better Be Home Soon

The telephone call with Officer Gray haunted me for weeks. One thing in particular continued to gnaw at me and kept me up nights: had other girls really come forward, as Officer Gray had implied? Or was that just a tactical investigative ploy to get me to sing? Had Tom been involved with other girls at school as well? Had he lied to me all this time, promising that I was the only one he had done something like this with?

I looked down at my journal, where I was writing, and adjusted my bedside lamp. It was midnight, and the world outside my window was pitch black. The edges of my room, beyond the circle of light, were a fuzzy gray, but promised no escape for my fevered mind. I felt as though I had no place to hide, and no safe haven. Worse, I had nothing to offer Tom – he was in the States alone, dealing with this mess that I had created. And he didn't even know how I really felt about him.

I leaned over my journal and continued writing my list of questions. Writing them down – making them physical – helped to get them out of my head, and had been helping me sleep, of late. I looked at the list now and gulped. It was getting quite long, and there were very few answers to go with the questions.

Would the charges against Tom be dropped, since I had given no incriminating testimony? Did Officer Gray believe my story? My friends and I often lied to our parents, about a number of large and small things, but lying to the police was something different. What if they doubted I was telling the truth because my testimony was so different from the other students? Would I be asked to take a polygraph test?

If there were other girls involved, had they already testified against Tom? Was it already too late?

November came and went, and without much celebration due to the tension at home. I finally left fifteen behind and turned sixteen. My dad organized a small party and my mom got me a colorful birthday cake, but after nearly three months in Chile I was in no mood for a celebration. Tom was constantly in my thoughts, my dreams, and even my prayers. Did he realize that I was turning sixteen? Did he even care? Did he hate me now that he knew I had told my friends about him? Did he think that I had told the police more about our affair? Was he in police custody? Did he lose his job at Royal Oaks?

The questions burned holes through my mind, and I found it hard to concentrate on anything else. With the stress from being stuck in limbo between education systems and the case involving Tom, I lost a lot of weight, leaving my already thin frame even thinner.

Finally, after we'd been in Chile for five months, my dad called a family meeting in the living room. He asked Tony and me to sit on the velvety green sofa, while my mom stood by his side.

"Well, we're in a difficult situation here," he told us in a grave tone. "If you two just continue like this, your lives will have no meaning here. We can't afford to send both of you to a private British or American school at this point, so there's not much else we can do. You're leaving us with one option: for all of us to return to the United States so that Tony, you can go to college and Isabel, you can finish high school. I don't see that you're leaving me much choice, though I find your actions both selfish and immature. If you don't take the equivalency exams next month, which you have both clearly refused to prepare for, we're just going to have to move back and - "

My dad suddenly stopped short; he stared blankly at the hardwood floor for a moment, then clutched at his chest and fell to his knees, gasping. Tony was the first to react. He jumped from the sofa and caught my dad before he hit the floor. My mom knelt down next to him, hysterically calling his name, trying to cradle him in her arms. I jumped up instinctively and called an ambulance.

151

Later, in the hospital, the doctor told us that my father had not suffered a heart attack, as we had thought. It had been a nervous breakdown. "It's the stress," my mother told us outside my father's hospital room. "It was his dream to start a new life here and now he can't, because his children won't let him. Why can't the both of you just bend a little? Is that too much to ask? Your father can't take much more of this."

As she walked back to my dad's bedside, Tony and I exchanged guilty looks. I felt terrible. We had been so absorbed in what we wanted that we never once cast a thought to how our choices were affecting our dad. We had both caused him such stress, which had driven him to a nervous breakdown.

"But what about the things we want?" Tony asked quietly. "They didn't ask *us* if we wanted this new life. They didn't ask us if we wanted to come here, leave all of our friends behind, lose everything we knew back home…" His voice faded away and he glanced at me, his brows drawn down in a frown.

I shook my head in mute response. I didn't know what to tell him, or even how to answer myself. I felt very guilty about what had happened to my dad, but I agreed with Tony; we hadn't been given a choice about this move, and deserved to make at least some of our own decisions. Weren't we allowed to live out our dreams as well?

The atmosphere in the house was even more chilled after my father returned from the hospital. No one seemed to want to speak to anyone else, for fear of what they would say, and the house became a virtual war zone. Tony and I hurried quickly back to our rooms after each uncomfortably silent meal, and emerged only when our parents left to investigate business opportunities the next morning. We spent more time together than we ever had, trying to find a solution to the problem, and failing. One late November morning, my dad walked into the living room where my brother and I were watching CNN.

"Here are your airplane tickets," he said in a curt voice, throwing an envelope down on the sofa in the space between where my brother and I were sitting. "You're both going back to California with your mother in a week."

Tony looked up at my dad. "What about you, Papi? Are you coming with us?"

"Me? You can forget about me for a while," my dad said brusquely. "This is where I want to be, and I'm staying right here. You can start packing. You won't be able to take all of your things either, so just take whatever can fit into two suitcases."

Before either of us could respond, my father turned and walked out through the front door. Tony and I looked at each other, confused at this dramatic change of course. Going back to the United States? This had never even been discussed as an option. With my mother but without him?

"He's breaking up our family?" I asked, confused. "Why would he do that? Why would he send us back?"

"He's upset because he doesn't want us to leave," Tony finally answered. "Isabel, we've really messed everything up for him … maybe we should stay, you know?"

"What about Amy?" I asked. "Don't you miss her? Don't you want to go back to be with her?"

"Of course I miss her," Tony responded without any hesitation. "But I've been doing a lot of thinking since Papi ended up in the hospital, and I think our family is more important than any girlfriend."

I stared at the envelope lying on the sofa, and thought about returning to California and living a normal life again. I missed my friends terribly, and I missed our lives there, but I missed Tom the most. That didn't mean that this was the right way to go, though. The right way would have been with both of my parents, as a happy and united family.

Finally I sighed and shook my head. "Papi's already bought our tickets, Tony. You know how he is once his mind is made up," I said quietly, looking at him. "I don't think we're going to have any choice in this. I think we should just go back."

Tony didn't reply, but later that night we both took our suitcases out and began to pack. My dad stood in my doorway for some time, watching, but didn't say a thing.

My uncle volunteered to drive us to the airport, and got to the house early in the morning for the trip. My dad stood quietly on the porch, watching, but did not volunteer to help us with our bags. He'd been ignoring us since he gave us the plane tickets, and acting as though we'd already left. Today he spoke only to my mom, who held onto his hand as if it were a lifeline. When my uncle arrived, he placed all of our bags into the trunk of the car. My father watched, then walked over to my mom and hugged her tightly, wiping tears from his eyes. When it was our turn to bid him farewell, he turned to us coldly, said, "Goodbye," and turned away again. There was no hug or kiss, and nothing to signify that he was sorry we were leaving. As soon as we got in the car, he walked back into the house and did not come out again.

I had a lump in my throat the size of a softball all the way from our house to the airport. The mood in the car was somber, and made worse by my uncle, who occasionally threw out barbed comments about Tony and I being selfish children, intent on ruining my dad's life.

Santiago International Airport seemed a much more desolate place now than it had when we first arrived. There were more travelers milling around, but the place seemed drab and depressing, and we had lost the excitement of embarking on a new adventure. I sat next to Tony in a corner of the departure lounge, near our corresponding gate. My mom was sitting alone, a few seats away, looking desolate, sad, and hopeless. She didn't tell us what she was thinking, but her disappointment was written over her entire face.

The first few days back in California were as difficult as they could have been. Back in Chile, I had never thought about what the move back to California would be like. Where would we live? Would we move back to our old neighborhood? How would my mom manage to pay the bills on her own, without my dad? None of these things ever crossed my mind; I had thought merely that "normal" life would be waiting for us when we returned.

In reality, life would not return to normal for a long time. We had to stay in a gloomy, run-down hotel until we found a house to rent; Tony practically moved into Amy's house, leaving me with my depressed mom in the dark and miserable hotel room. We didn't see Tony for days at a time, and I couldn't bear to go off with my friends and leave my mom by herself. So I stayed, trying to keep her from sliding any deeper into her depression.

In all my years, I had never witnessed my mother break down. She had always been the backbone of the family, the force that bound everyone together. My father had been nearly useless without her, and we'd always gone to her first with our problems and joys. She had been our strength. Now, my mother wouldn't eat, wouldn't get out of bed, and wouldn't respond to my questions. She was trapped in her own world of sorrow, sadness, and heartbreak, and I couldn't find a way to soothe her or make things better. I couldn't leave her; I was afraid that if I left her alone, she would do something rash, like try to take her own life. As I worried about my mom's welfare and health, I obsessed about Tom. How could I contact him now that I was back? Should I call him at home? Was the case with the police over or was it ongoing? Could I find him at Royal Oaks? Would he even want to talk to me? My mind was muddled with confusion and my chest ached from the emotional roller coaster that had become my life.

"Isabel, what are we doing here?" my mom asked me one day as we lay in the queen-sized bed together. "We should be back in Santiago with your dad. We deserted him, and now he's all alone. You know that your dad can't be alone. He's a family man without a family now, and it's our fault."

"Mami, don't worry," I murmured, stroking her untidy hair gently, trying to soothe the restless mind inside. "Papi will come back to us soon. He's angry and hurt right now, but once he cools off a little bit, he'll realize how much he misses us. He'll come back. You know he can't be away from us for long. Now, we need to get you dressed so we can find a house to rent. You don't want Papi to come back and find us in a hotel, do you?"

I had learned that there was one thing I could do to snap my mom out of her moments of despair; any time I mentioned my dad, she responded. She already felt that she'd disappointed and deserted him, and she wasn't willing to make things any worse. I'd learned to use that as a spur to get her moving, and I hoped to use it to get us a house. My mom had Chilean family friends in Hillside, and they had promised to help me get my mom back on her feet. She and I had most of our meals at their house, to keep our strength up, and they encouraged her to move back into work. After weeks of trying, I finally convinced my mom to begin contacting her former clients again. As a financial advisor, she had been very successful in California and I was sure her clients would be happy she had returned. The work was good for her, since it gave her something to think about other than my father's loneliness. It also forced her out into the world, and she brightened with the additional exposure. Once she had enough work to pay all of the bills and keep us a little more secure, we rented a three-bedroom house in a quiet little neighborhood very close to Royal Oaks. Tony re-emerged from his time with Amy, and we began to rebuild our family. My father's place was still empty, though, and we all felt that void profoundly.

Chapter Thirteen

Believe

*L*ife didn't fully return to normal until I started attending school again. This was what I had missed most in Chile, and represented a return to social activity and learning. There were some obstacles; I'd been gone for three full months of the school year, and had missed the first term of school, so couldn't return to my previous high school. If I wanted to return to regular high school and begin classes in February when the second semester began, I had to enroll in continuation school - where trouble students earned their high school degree equivalents - to make up the course material I'd missed.

I was determined to get through it, and I didn't have much else to do, so I worked hard. Within three weeks of enrolling in the continuation school, I had made up all the required coursework. I even had two weeks to spare before the second semester began. My mom was delighted with my progress, and asked to talk to me about what came next.

"So Isabel, we need to get you back to Royal Oaks and enroll you in the second semester," she said as she drove me home on the last day of class at the continuation school. "We should do it this week since classes begin next month."

I paused. I was happy to see my mother engaged and driving, and I didn't want to disappoint her, but I'd already decided on this issue. "Mami, I was thinking that maybe I wouldn't attend Royal Oaks again," I said cautiously. "Maybe I could attend West End High School instead. It's a few blocks further from the house, but West End is much better academically. And if I want to go to a good college..."

"But, I thought you liked Royal Oaks," my mom responded, surprised. "Don't all your friends go there? Don't you want to swim and play basketball again? You've got a year and a half left, don't you want to graduate with your friends?"

"Yeah, but I also want more of an academic challenge," I quickly replied, casting about for as many reasons I could think of. "West End might give me a better chance of getting into a good college. I need to think about taking college prep classes and I've heard West End has a great college prep curriculum. My friends from Royal Oaks all live close by, so I'll still get to hang out with them anytime I want."

My mom frowned, unconvinced. "Well it's your choice, I suppose," she responded, and I breathed a sigh of relief. "We'll go to West End tomorrow morning and see what it would take to enroll you there."

Liz, however, was aghast at my decision to enroll at West End. I met her the next day to talk to her about it in person.

"Isabel, are you crazy? Do you really want to go to a new high school at this stage? It's junior year. Izzy, we graduate next year! Don't you want to graduate with all of us, all of your old friends? You know that you won't make friends like us at West End, it's just too late in the game!"

"But after what happened with Tom and everything, how could I show my face there again?" I asked. I'd thought about this quite a bit, and had come to the decision that it would be best for me to avoid my past as much as possible. "It would be so awkward and I'd feel so uncomfortable. There would be so much gossip. Everyone would look at me from the corners of their eyes and whisper to each other, 'Hey, isn't that the girl who slept with Mr. Stevens? Isn't she the one that got him in trouble? What's she doing back here?' or 'Look, that's the girl who started all that trouble for Mr. Stevens. She must be a real slut.' And what if the police decide to reopen the case because I'm back in town?"

Although moving to Chile had been a nightmare, I was convinced that it had indirectly kept Tom out of prison and me out of trouble. I thought that Sarah's mind had been made up. She was going to send that letter regardless of whether I was here or not. If the police got the letter when I was still in town, they would have followed both Tom and I. They would have staked out the entire mountain, for all I knew, and put under-cover cops at the high school. We would have been caught, eventually, and Tom would have been charged, convicted, and thrown into prison for a long, long time.

My absence had kept that from happening, and I was determined to maintain that distance – and ensure Tom's safety – regardless of what it did to my social life or my emotions.

"Isabel, no matter what has gone on, no one can stop you from enrolling at Royal Oaks," Liz said, sounding frustrated. "Even Principal Warren can't do that. You didn't do anything wrong. Anyway, no one is really talking about it anymore. It's old news. Mr. Stevens is back at school teaching, so the case must be closed."

I sighed. Liz was right; I'd done some research when I got back in town, and knew that the police had failed to find any direct evidence against Tom. I had refused to cooperate, and I was the only student involved. They couldn't prosecute the man based on another student's handwritten letter, no matter how damning it was. His wife had testified that nothing had changed, and that they'd even gone on a two-week camping trip with the family over the summer. The police had been forced to release Tom and drop the charges. His name had been cleared, though I was sure that many parents didn't want him at the school, and he'd gone back to teaching.

I was terrified of seeing him, though, and worried about his reaction if he saw me on campus again. I was afraid that he would be angry with me, possibly even think that I had been the one to turn him in. He might believe that I had come back upset, with the intention of settling a score with him. Worse, he might believe that I was back in California to assist the police in their criminal case against him. I had never sent him the letter I wrote, where I explained my sudden disappearance from his life, and he probably wondered what was going on in my head or how I felt about him. It wouldn't take much for him to react to my presence with anger or betrayal. For my sake and Tom's, it seemed best that I attend another school, where no one knew my name or, more importantly, my past.

"I don't know, Liz," I said looking down at the brand new carpet that lined my new bedroom. "It's just risky, I think. Everyone will be gossiping about me, and I'll feel so uncomfortable. I mean, do I really need that right now? And what about Tom? How would he react? Don't you think I would be selfish if I didn't consider his feelings? He might not want to see me there."

Liz growled in frustration. "Isabel, don't let what happened ruin your life. Just put it in the past where it belongs and move on. Royal Oaks is where you should be. Even if some people gossip about it, and ask stupid questions, just deny everything and don't worry about it." She reached over and grabbed my arm, her fingers cold on my warm sweater sleeve.

"I promise you, it'll only be uncomfortable for the first day or two, if that, and then it'll be business as usual. And I'll be with you. Your friends will take care of you."

I looked at her, conflicted. There were just so many things to think about. Of *course* I wanted to return to Royal Oaks, be with my old friends, and enjoy the last year and a half of high school, but there was a nagging voice inside my head, telling me over and over again that it was a bad idea. Was I over reacting? Being paranoid? Liz was so sure that it would be okay...

"Well, I guess it would make sense for me to go to Royal Oaks," I finally answered quietly. "It's much closer to my house and it would be nice to be back in a familiar place, with my friends. But if I feel totally weird there after the first week, you know, if people are saying things and talking behind my back, then I'm out of there."

"If things get out of hand, I'll step in and back you up," Liz promised. "You know that I know almost everyone at school. And your other friends will do the same, I know it. Trust me, you'll be fine. Just come back, Isabel."

Liz's unwavering pressure convinced me to go back to Royal Oaks, and my mom re-enrolled me the following day. Destiny – or Liz's conviction – led me back to that high school, and inevitably back to Tom.

Chapter Fourteen

Why Does My Heart Feel So Bad?

*A*s I walked down the open-air, concrete corridors of Royal Oaks on the first day of the new term, I realized that a new inmate walking through the prison courtyard must feel very much the same. I was vulnerable and guarded, waiting for disaster to strike at any moment. The halls were lined with familiar posters, clinging to the brick walls with silver duct tape. This time, they were advertising the upcoming Valentine's Day dance in bright purple handwriting. I saw the same buildings around me, and familiar faces everywhere; people I'd known for years.

But nothing appeared friendly.

I was overwhelmed and my stomach was tied up into hundreds of tiny knots. I had Liz next to me, but I knew that she would have to go to her first period class soon. We didn't have that class together, and that meant that I would be alone, fending for myself, in about five minutes. I watched the students rushing by me, and wondered what they thought of me; none of them were glancing my way, and I wondered if I was truly that anonymous. Was the gnawing fear I felt merely a product of my hyperactive imagination? Had everyone truly forgotten, as Liz said they had? My old friends came over to greet me excitedly, and I began to breathe again. No one said anything about Tom. People were not staring at me. In fact, no one was really paying attention to me at all. Maybe the police hadn't told anyone outside my immediate circle of friends that I was the student involved in 'the case'. Perhaps Liz was right, and everything would be okay. I left Liz and strode toward my first class, feeling confident for the first time in months.

No amount of comfort and normality could have prepared me for seeing Tom again, though it had to happen at some point. We crossed paths just after lunch, outside his classroom. I was walking by, rushing toward my next class, and hadn't realized I would be walking past his classroom. He stood at the door, watching the students walk by, with a textbook in his hand. He was speaking to one of his students, laughing at something she had said, when I saw him. I stopped dead, like a deer caught in bright headlights in the dead of night, then cringed and quickly turned away. I knew my cheeks were flushed, and my heart raced in my chest; I couldn't turn around and face Tom, not like this, not in front of everyone.

Out of the corner of my eye I saw that Tom had looked at me then turned away. He didn't appear surprised or seem to care that I was there. When I looked back, he had disappeared into his classroom.

Just after I returned to Royal Oaks in February, my dad returned to join us. We had all known that he wouldn't be able to stay in Santiago on his own, and it wasn't a surprise when he returned. It wasn't that he couldn't do his own laundry or prepare his own meals, but he was a family man at heart and simply missed us. All in all, we spent just over two months as a fatherless family in California.

Tony started his journey toward adult life at this time, working hard to juggle college classes and work. He began working at a local fast food restaurant, despite his heavy class load, and made a point of paying for his own things, like car insurance and gas.

"Tony, you're killing yourself," I said one day. He had come in to have breakfast with me, and his face alone was enough to cause worry. He was paler than I'd ever seen him, with dark circles under puffy eyes, and his mouth was pinched with fatigue.

He shook his head. "I'm more tired than I've ever been, but it's worth it. Dad needs to see that I can provide for myself. He needs to see that I'm an adult now, and can make my own decisions." He paused. "I don't want him to think that we came back here for nothing. I want him to know that it was worthwhile, and that we appreciate it."

I frowned. "You know, Tony, you could just tell him so. You don't have to tear yourself apart demonstrating it."

He grinned at me. "That wouldn't be nearly as much fun. Besides, saying it doesn't make it true. *Doing* it makes it true."

I watched him walk away, and thought about his words. He was right, really. He'd enrolled in classes at a community college, in a program that would lead him to a four-year university, and had already been promoted to manager at the fast food restaurant. My dad was so impressed with Tony's progress and newfound sense of responsibility that he surprised him with a secondhand VW Golf. The fact that they were on speaking terms again had been progress, and my dad's pride had been twice as valuable to Tony, given the events of the past year.

My dad, for his part, had softened with the time apart. He'd missed us badly after we left Chile, and had come back to the U.S. with a gentler heart. We'd discussed the situation as a family, and had all agreed that everyone was at least partially at fault. We'd also decided, though, that it was best to go forward as a family again, and with everyone's best interests in mind. It was a brand new attitude from my father, who had always played ruling patriarch, and Tony and I were making the most of it.

As part of the new agreement, my dad had decided that it was time for me to learn to drive. As old fashioned as he was, my dad insisted that I learn to drive on his manual transmission pick-up truck.

"Driving a stick shift will make you a better and more conscientious driver, trust me," he muttered, showing me into the driver's side.

"I'm not sure I want to be either," I joked, looking from the steering wheel to the stick shift, and experimenting with the clutch and brake. I'd seen people driving, of course, but I'd never considered the possibility that I might learn to do it so soon. We'd always planned to move to Chile before I turned sixteen, so I would have learned there rather than here.

Now, everything had changed. My dad and I spent the next three weeks struggling with the learning process. I couldn't get the timing of clutch in-shift-clutch out, and stalled the truck every time we came to a stop or a hill. I even managed to stall the truck on the freeway once, which led to an alarming episode of my dad jumping into the driver's seat, pushing me out of the way, and taking over. After that, we stayed on small residential streets until I got the hang of it.

In the end, it was all worth it. Within weeks of getting my driver's permit, my dad took me car shopping.

"A belated birthday present," he told me, smiling tenderly. "I wasn't in the best mood on your birthday, and I don't think you would have accepted anything from me in any case."

I smiled at him, wondering at the change, and looked around us. We were at a used car lot, "seeing what was out there," as my dad told me. We looked at a couple of cars in the row, then found a small, sporty gray Honda Civic. It boasted a sun roof and of course, manual transmission. We took one look at the car, then looked at each other and nodded. My father pulled cash out of his pocket and paid the dealership then and there, and I drove the car home. I was the first one in my group of friends to own a car, and the only sixteen year old in my class who drove herself to school. I couldn't have been happier.

The car gave me status and easy transportation, and provided some valuable opportunities for movement. I was responsible for my own transportation, now, and didn't have to ask anyone to take me anywhere. I used that to put myself in the right places at the right times. I'd started paying close attention to Tom and his movements the second week of school, and knew his new schedule. I pinpointed his whereabouts between periods, and watched where he went before and after school. I couldn't help myself; I knew that it was a bad idea, but missed him terribly, and wanted to know how he was doing. I was dying to talk to him, but made sure that I was never seen close to him.

I was careful, though, and went out of my way to avoid walking through areas of the campus where we might run into each other. I always walked the other way if I saw him coming toward me. I realized that every teacher on campus knew my name, and wondered if they'd been told to stay away from me. I became convinced that they were all watching me, and waiting for me to slip up and be seen with Tom. In return, I became determined to lie low and stay out of Tom's way. The last thing I wanted was for a member of faculty, or the students, to see Tom and me within 5 feet of each other.

The truth was, though, that I still ached to run to Tom and hide in his arms, to bury my face in his chest, and to inhale his familiar clean-laundry scent. There were so many things wrong about our former relationship, but I felt that if we were together, we would make it right. At least he would make me feel safe. After all the time that had gone by, I was still completely enamored with him, and missed him a great deal. Because of our situation, though, all I could do was enjoy the sights I caught of him walking to and from his classroom. I tried not to look at him too often on campus, but I found a way to do so from the safety and privacy of my car.

Every morning, I picked Liz up from her house and gave her a ride to school. I had been late in my enrollment, and was stuck with a retail sales class for first and second period, which meant that I didn't actually have to be on campus until third period, since my retail sales class and practicum was in a department store at the local shopping mall. Regardless, I picked Liz up from home in the morning, dropped her off on campus, lingered about in the parking lot and then drove myself to the shopping mall for my practicum.

"You're really nice drive me to school, you know," Liz muttered the first day. "Though I think it's just an excuse for you to drive your new car."

I laughed along with her, but grew serious as I drove slowly onto the school parking lot. Liz knew as well as I did that I had ulterior motives for driving her; her house was out of the way, and going to school before first period added a full twenty minutes to my morning commute. It was worth it, though; I pulled up to the curb in the parking lot to drop her off, and glanced quickly around the lot.

"Looking for anyone in particular?" she teased quietly, leaning down to go through her bag.

"You know I am," I smiled back. "He's not here yet, though."

Liz laughed, shaking her head. Two times out of three, we got there just in time to catch Tom driving up, parking, and walking from his truck to his classroom. I was more comfortable watching him from my car, since I had tinted windows and left school quickly after he left the parking lot. When I was parked waiting for Liz to gather her things and get to class, I could watch him from a safe distance, observe what he was wearing, how he'd cut his hair, and try to decipher his mood. I didn't have to worry about who was around me or whether other people were watching me watching him, because it was unlikely.

"You know it's a bad idea," Liz said, growing serious. "Of course I want you to be happy, but you guys have already been in trouble. If I can identify you from outside your car, then everyone else can as well. And that includes Mr. Stevens. Are you *trying* to get caught again?"

"Shush," I answered, though I knew that she was right. I was playing with fire, and the last thing I actually wanted to do was get caught. I couldn't help myself, though; this was the only opportunity I had to interact with him, even if nothing actually happened between us. "Maybe I *want* him to know that I'm watching."

I still had no idea how Tom felt about me after all that had transpired. Did he think I knew about the letter that Sarah had written to Mrs. Drake? Did he think that I'd had something to do with that? I hoped not; I hoped that he had more faith in me than that, and that he would believe, truly believe, that the whole incident was just something that got out of hand. I felt awful for my role in it – my carelessness and the blind faith I'd had in my friend. I wanted and needed Tom to understand that I didn't mean any harm, that no matter what happened, I had never wanted to hurt him, and especially not in this way. I was hoping that I'd run into him and that the run-in would give us a chance to talk, at some point, and clear things up.

If I was being honest, though, I was also hoping that it would give us a chance to talk about whether we still had feelings for each other.

"Well, I can't stay much longer," Liz said, breaking into my thoughts. "I have to be in class early this morning, to get ready for an exam." She turned in the seat, craning her neck to look at the parking lot behind us. "Ah," she muttered, "he's here. That's my cue." She turned to me with a serious face, and frowned a bit. "Please try to be careful, Izzy. Don't talk to him, and at least try to hide a bit. There are other teachers around, and they're all on the lookout for anything suspicious."

"I know, Liz, I know," I answered quickly. "I just want to see if he looks at me. I want to know if he's pissed off at me."

Liz shrugged, then opened the door and climbed out. She shut the door without a word, and I turned to my mirror to watch Tom walk by. Today, he was dressed in a sharp pair of dress pants and a dark button up shirt, and he looked terrific. He was also walking closer to my car than he had in the past. I frowned. He lengthened his stride, as though he was trying to catch up to Liz, but then turned toward my car instead. I never expected him to get so close, and I didn't know what to do. I could duck further into my seat, he was standing right next to my car and there was nowhere to hide.

He was suddenly at my window, his face level with mine. His hazel eyes looked softer than ever, framed by what seemed to be years of worry and stress. A huge lump formed in my throat and my heart raced in panic. What was he thinking? Was he completely insane? He couldn't just come up to me like this. What would people say? Did he want to go to prison?

He reached out and tapped on my window, his mouth turning up in a shy smile. I fumbled for the button and rolled my window down, looking at him in question. He leaned on my doorframe and looked into my eyes.

"What is it, Isabel?" he asked casually. "I've seen you parked here every morning. Do you need something?"

"Are you mad?" I hissed. "You shouldn't be coming up to me like this. What if someone sees us?"

Surprisingly, Tom smiled, exposing his perfectly straight set of teeth. The goatee he wore on his face was still well groomed, but his dirty blonde hair had grown out a bit and his temples sported more silver than I remembered, giving him a more rugged, distinguished look. *He's never looked better*, I thought.

"Isabel, I wasn't charged with anything," he replied, as if the whole case were merely a trifle, like a speeding ticket or a parking fine. "Besides, I don't think talking to you is a crime. They can hardly prosecute me for trying to help a student with something."

"I don't want to sound insulting," I whispered nervously. "But I don't think this is very smart of you. Maybe you weren't charged with anything, but I think the police can still draw conclusions. Especially if they see us talking."

Tom chuckled.

"Isabel, no one can do anything to me unless *you* turn me in," he replied. "It's as simple as that. And since we're on the subject - and finally talking - I wanted to thank you for protecting me. Your testimony was the only thing that kept me here at school ... and out of court. Thank you for staying quiet. You have no idea what that meant to me." He was nervous as he spoke, although he tried to make light of the situation.

I felt a familiar rush of blood to the face, and looked down, confused and embarrassed. "You're welcome," I replied quietly, my cheeks burning. "I hope you know that I'd never do anything to hurt you. I hoped that you knew it wasn't me, who turned you in." Just then, I saw another teacher arriving at the far end of the parking lot, and panicked. "Look, I should go. This might look suspicious and I don't want to get you into any more trouble."

Tom stepped back.

"All right, you don't want to be late for your next class," he said, straightening. I fumbled for the button to roll up the window, but stopped when he added, "Isabel?"

I looked up, locking eyes with him. He held my gaze.

"I'm glad you're back," he said, and gave me one of his genuine, broad smiles. It was so infectious and irresistible that I couldn't help grinning back.

"Yeah, me too," I said. I grew serious, then rolled up my window and sped away.

Chapter Fifteen

Losing My Religion

I spent the rest of the morning in a daze. James, the main shift supervisor for my retail training class, stopped me while I was removing the protective film from the new inventory in the basement.

"Isabel?" he asked quietly, "Are you with me this morning?"

I blinked, looking up at him. "What is it, James? Am I doing something wrong?"

He shook his head, frowning. "No, you're not doing anything wrong, but I can see you're having a bad day. What's up? Are you okay? You seem like you're on auto-pilot or something."

I forced a smile and looked down at the clothes on the table in front of me. At twenty-two, James was the youngest supervisor we had. Most of the girls in my course had a crush on him, with his dimples and brawny physique. He stood 6 feet tall, and had the body of a football player, with soft brown eyes framed by thick black, curly lashes. The other girls in the class would be terribly jealous of the personal attention he was giving me.

"Thanks, James, I'm fine. Just thinking about some stuff, that's all. You're sweet to ask, though."

"That's what I like about you." James shifted slightly to help me with the heavier clothes on the rack. His movement put him closer to me and I was happy for the help. "You're young but you're down to earth. You don't behave like girls your age at all. I'm sure I'm not the first one who's noticed that you've got both brains and beauty."

I looked at him, surprised. It was odd to hear James talk so personally like this; he was engaged to one of the women in the department store, and he usually carried himself very professionally. The personal attention he was showing me was flattering and I felt as though I was the object of James' desires.

"I don't know, not really," I laughed, trying to shrug it off. "I mean, people don't really come up to me and tell me they think I'm smart and attractive. It's just not that common, you know?"

James gave me a wry smile. "I thought you'd have noticed that I always come into your Monday morning classes, on the days you don't work on the main floor." His shoulder nudged up against mine as he reached over for the rest of the inventory, the soft hair on his skin brushing up against my exposed arm. James whispered, "And here I thought I was being too obvious."

I stared at him, caught off guard by what he was sharing. I felt the heat rise through my cheeks as I smiled, revealing my newly straightened and brace-less teeth. "I don't know what to say, James. I'm kind of surprised. I never noticed you were paying extra attention to me," I said shyly, still putting clothes on the display racks.

The situation was completely inappropriate, not merely because he was my supervisor, but also because he was engaged to a woman who was working in the same building and was, in fact, on the premises at this very moment. "James, we should stop talking here," I said quickly, stepping away from him and the display racks. "There are a whole lot of students over there, and they're probably wondering why we're whispering like this."

James' eyes flickered down to my light green button-up blouse that was practically painted on my torso before he met my gaze. I brought my hand to my chest, feeling exposed, and suddenly wondered what I'd been thinking, wearing this type of blouse. It was obviously too tight.

"Yeah, let's talk outside of the store, after your shift," he said quietly, leaning toward me. "You have about another month here and you're finished with this retail training course, right? Maybe we could get together after that?"

I stared into his dark eyes, surprised. He glanced down my body at my legs, and then back up, and I suppressed a smile. I couldn't help but stare at his warm brown eyes, perfectly lined by thick, dark lashes. "Yep, that's about right, one more month to go," I answered confidently. I took another step back, to put some distance between us. "Maybe we can catch up after school is out," I said nonchalantly, still in awe by the words spilling from my mouth. What was I thinking? James was handsome and sweet, but how could I have just placed myself in yet another compromising situation? My cheeks still burned from my nervous blush.

James' fleshy pink lips parted into a smile exposing two perfect dimples on his cheeks. "Sounds good, Isabel. I'll get your number when we finish up here and we can make some plans," he said as he began to way away in a confident stride. "Keep up the good work," James quipped from afar, sending one of his radiant smiles my way before turning the corner and disappearing.

Vicky began bullying me into joining the swim team again, and by the time sign-ups rolled around in early January; I was ready to join the team just to shut her up. The first couple of practices were uneventful and boring; my real joy on the team had been my interactions with Tom, but he was no longer allowed to coach the swim team. We had a new female coach instead.

"Why can't Mr. Stevens coach anymore?" I asked Vicky one afternoon as we dried off in the locker room after practice.

She looked at me, aghast. "Are you kidding? You don't know why he can't coach?"

"I've heard some things, Vicky, but I was out of the country for the beginning of the school year, remember? I don't know all the gossip."

She looked at me, and then shrugged nonchalantly. "Well, Mr. Stevens can't coach because he was suspected of having inappropriate relationships with students, some of which were his swimmers from last season," she replied, looking straight at me. "I'm sure you know *that*, since you were one of the students named."

I shrugged back, wearing an unconcerned look on my face. "Yeah, but nothing ever came of it. I talked to the police and told them that nothing happened. And he was never charged with anything, so if he's still teaching here, why can't he coach? It doesn't make any sense to me."

Vicky waved her hand dismissively. "No, they didn't charge him, but a lot of people still think he's guilty. Principal Warren still has his eye on him, so he's restricted his ability to coach swimming."

"Interesting," I said through gritted teeth. "So much for innocent until proven guilty, huh?"

The thought of Tom being banned from coaching infuriated me, because I knew how much he had enjoyed working with the swim team, and I knew that it was my fault he'd been banned from doing so. This was an unspoken guilty verdict, and proof that everyone believed we'd done what the police alleged. No wonder all the teachers looked at me the way they did. It was a wonder that Tom could still teach at Royal Oaks; he must know what his colleagues thought of him, and recognize the accusing looks of the other teachers. During the remainder of swim season, I swam without motivation, passion, or interest. My body propelled me forward, but I had no heart or enthusiasm for the sport. Tom sometimes stopped by the meets to help with timekeeping and these were my only exciting moments on the swim team.

Since I couldn't see Tom at practice, I found other ways to do so. The situation with James had been disturbing, but had led me to some very important conclusions. James was only twenty-two – almost my age, and far more appropriate in regard to dating – but he'd made me feel like an object and as if I had no voice or decision-making capacity, something Tom never did. His eyes had suggested terrible things, and I'd left the department store early on many occasions to stop off at home and immediately shower before going to school for third period. I'd also made sure that my records didn't include my home phone number, since I didn't want him reaching me outside of the department store. I stayed away from him during first and second period from then on, and went out of my way to leave the space we shared if I could.

Tom, on the other hand, had always been kind, forgiving, and thoughtful. He was many years older than James and myself, but had treated me with admiration and respect, and more like an equal. He'd never frightened me or made me feel uncomfortable in his presence, and certainly never made me feel unsafe. The experience with James – and the emotions it brought up – just made me more determined to find a new common ground with Tom.

My morning drop offs at the school parking lot had been the first step in the development of a secret language that only Tom and I shared. Now, with every appearance, I knew that Tom was trying to speak to me, trying to let me know that he still cared, and most of all, that his heart still ached for me.

During one of our final home meets of the season, Tom showed up again as an official timekeeper. Rather than leaving silently after the meet concluded, as he had done in the past, he lingered behind. I watched him, wondering what he was up to. There were only a few people left on the concrete deck near the pool, and I made sure that I was one of them. Natalie and I lingered at the concrete benches that surrounded the deck, putting our things away slowly and discussing where we were going to go after the meet. I was making every effort to stay behind because it was clear to me that Tom was trying to get my attention.

"Come on, Isabel, are you ready?" Natalie asked finally. She put her flip-flops on and flung her swim bag over her shoulder.

I glanced in Tom's general direction; he was standing just outside the main gate of the pool, near the girls' locker room.

"Sure," I replied. "Let's go."

We walked toward the gate, still wearing our wet bathing suits and furry parkas, drying our hair with our towels. I'd already decided that I was going to head straight home to take a shower, and was in the midst of telling Natalie that she was invited over when she noticed Tom standing at the gate.

"Hey, Mr. Stevens, what's up?" she called out, smiling. All the swimmers had loved Tom when he was our coach, but they'd also jumped on the bandwagon when he was investigated. Natalie was one of the only girls on the team who didn't talk about him like he was a criminal. "You know, it really sucks to be on the swim team this year. Aren't you coming back? It's no fun swimming for this team anymore."

Tom smiled wryly. "I'm sure it's not that bad, Natalie. At least you've got your buddies to keep you company, and keep you laughing. I'm sure you and Isabel are still managing to have a good time."

Tom's reference to me made me smile on impulse, and he turned his gaze toward me. His eyes looked brighter than ever, the sunlight diminishing his pupils to tiny black spots engulfed by a sea of tranquil greenish-brown.

"So," he said, "how were your races, Isabel?"

Seeing that Tom was there to talk to me rather than her, Natalie waved at us both as she walked toward the girls' locker room, just steps away. "I'm going to have a shower, Iz," she called, plunging through the door. "I'll meet you afterwards."

Tom and I both stood and watched as she disappeared into the brick building's main entrance. When she was gone, I turned back to him.

"I see your friend can take a hint," Tom said as he stepped closer to me. "Does Natalie know something, or is she just in a hurry to leave?"

"No, she doesn't know a thing. My days of telling my friends any secrets are over, you can be sure of that." I felt my body slowly inching closer to Tom, as if pulled by some over-powering magnetic attraction, until I was finally standing no more than a foot away from him. "So what're you doing here? I mean, it's not really smart for us to be seen talking like this."

Tom's demeanor changed, and he suddenly became completely serious. His brows drew down in a frown. "You're right, but I've tried, and I can't hide from you. I've tried - for months now - not to notice you. As usual, you're much better at this than I am. You're doing a wonderful job at ignoring me, and going on with your life. You're so good at it that it hurts. I know it's for the best, but I just can't do the same." He looked up at me, hoping to see a look of understanding on my face as he waited for my response.

I swallowed, wishing I knew what to say. Tom's words frightened me, but their truth tore at my heart. We were so close to trouble, so close to jail time, but when he was around I had trouble taking that seriously. I wanted to smell his familiar scent again, I wanted to feel the touch of his hands on my skin, feel his hair against my cheek, and feel that goatee of his bristling on my skin. These were all bad ideas, though, and I was very aware that we were being watched.

I cleared my throat and redirected my gaze towards my thin feet in their black rubber flip-flops. "I miss talking to you, too," I confessed. "I wanted to write you a letter, but I didn't know if it would be a good idea. Look maybe you could give me a call at home instead – "

"No, I'd rather talk to you face to face," Tom interrupted. "Can you come to my classroom tomorrow before third period? Just for five minutes?"

My heart raced. "Isn't that dangerous? Should I be coming into your classroom? What would people think?"

"Isabel, relax," Tom said, an edge of frustration in his tone. "Nothing's going to happen if we're careful. I don't have a third period, so there won't be any students in my classroom. Just stop by for a few minutes before you head to your third period class, can you do that for me?"

Of course I could do that for him, of course I could do that for me, of course I could do that for us, I thought, trying to convince myself that it would be okay. A small voice in my head shouted out a warning, but I pushed it down and nodded.

"All right," I finally replied. "I'll stop by tomorrow."

"Great." Tom broke into a relieved smile. "Now you'd better get going. I'm sure your friends are all waiting for you to give them rides home, you little taxi driver. I'll see you tomorrow."

I smiled back at him, and then ducked my head and quickly headed toward the girls' locker room.

My thoughts got the best of me that night, and all I could manage to do was toss and turn in bed, waiting for the hours to pass. Dozens of questions rushed through my head: what did Tom want to say to me that was so important that it had to be said face to face and not over the phone? Did he think that maybe his phone was tapped? Could *my* phone be tapped? Would the police department go to such lengths to come to the truth? Once a case was closed, could it be reopened just because one of the alleged victims was back in the country? What if the police department, with the permission of the school administration, had tapped Tom's classroom, so they decipher who came in and out, and what was said?

The idea of my most intimate conversations with Tom being caught on tape, exposed to the police and eventually to the world, sent shivers up my spine. If Tom and I were exposed, my father's heart would be broken. He would know that I had looked him straight in the eye and lied to him about having an affair with a married teacher. Worse, Tom could be charged and face jail time, and I would lose him forever. Maybe I should be more careful, I thought, and refuse to meet him. My heart yearned to be alone with Tom, though, to redis-cover those moments that we shared in that classroom of his, and I told myself that everything would be okay.

I spent much of my retail training class the next morn-ing prepping myself for my third-period meeting with Tom. I stripped the cellophane off the new inventory in the ware-house then walked quickly toward the perfume department.

The department store didn't open until ten in the morning, and the perfume department was empty.

I found an endless array of oddly shaped bottles of perfume on the shelves, waiting for customers to come in for samples. These were the "try me" bottles, and were already opened and ready for spraying. I inspected each shelf, carefully sniffing the lid of the bottles that caught my attention. After sniffing several bottles, I decided to go with a vanilla-scented, delicately shaped perfume bottle that rested comfortably in the palm of my hand. Vanilla was not one of my favorite scents, but I'd read somewhere that older men reacted positively to the scent of vanilla.

I misted myself generously with the perfume, taking the time to spray the scent over my hair and the nape of my neck. By the time I was finished, my white, fitted jeans and beige tank top, along with my long hair and skin, smelled lightly and pleasantly of vanilla.

I was on my way back to the room that served as our classroom, to gather my things, when James stepped out from behind a rack of clothes.

"Hey, Isabel, slow down," he called out.

My first thought was that he'd seen me spraying on the perfume, and I slowed and pulled back. Before I had a chance to speak, though, he reached for my hand and pulled me toward him. I held my breath, struck by his possessiveness of me in such a public, and potentially dangerous place.

"Morning, princess," he said with a smile. "You look like you're on a mission today; I could hardly catch up with you. Where are you going?"

"I'm sorry, James, I don't have time to talk today," I stuttered, my mind racing as I noticed all of James' perfect masculine features. "We have an exam and I want to spend some time studying before class. I think the others are already waiting for me."

James frowned and let go of my hand. "Oh, all right. You'd better go, then, if they're waiting for you. Good luck on your exam, Isabel," he said, winking at me and revealing those adorable dimples.

I nodded, a mischievous smile on my face, and rushed toward the elevator. Class would be out in five minutes, and I wanted to be in my car and driving by the time the other students left the department store. I ran by the classroom, gathered my things, and sprinted toward my car in the parking lot. The customers were starting to arrive, so I was anonymous through the small crowd that gathered at the main door, as I left early. I opened the door to my car, jumped in, and sped away for my meeting with Tom.

I slowed as I approached the campus, and tried to smooth my hair a bit. If I were late to Tom's class, then I would have less time to spend with him, and I didn't want to lose even a fraction of the time we would have alone. There was no way I could be late to third period; every teacher knew who I was now, because of the scandal, and I didn't want any of them asking why I was late. Any instance could lead to assumptions, and assumptions could lead to more inquiries, which could lead Tom and I down a path that would end will nothing but trouble.

I also didn't want to be seen rushing onto campus, though, as that could lead to more suspicions. I was walking a very fine line, with danger on both sides.

My nerves tingled and burned as I tried to stride casually toward Tom's classroom. I kept my steps quick but careless, hoping that I looked like any other high school student on her way to third period. The hall was crowded, as usual, and I kept my eyes down until I turned into the right hall. I reached the heavy metal door of Tom's classroom, took a moment to prepare myself for what lay ahead, as I reached out to turn the knob. I opened the door slightly, just wide enough for my body to fit, and slipped through. I closed the door quietly behind me.

To my surprise, Tom's classroom was completely vacant. I took a few careful steps toward the darkroom, and quietly called out, "Hello? Anyone there?"

No answer.

In a louder voice, I tried again, "Anyone? Hello?"

Nothing.

I gulped. Precious time was ticking away. Had Tom changed his mind? Was I being set up? Was he gone, or in trouble somewhere? By my calculations, I had about four minutes left before I needed to walk to the other end of the campus for my third period class. That didn't give me much time, and there was one place I hadn't looked yet. I turned and walked boldly into the darkroom, my hands in front of me feeling my way through the darkness.

Once inside, the familiar smell of developing chemicals hit me like a ton of bricks, and a flood of emotions took over. This dark chamber with its chemical scent represented something special to me: the beginnings of my relationship with Tom, and many of our initial romantic encounters. This was where it had all started, and this scent would always remind me of that.

I suddenly felt someone's hand take hold of my arm gently. Caught off guard, afraid, and unable to see who was there, I let out a soft gasp.

"It's me, Isabel. Don't worry. We're completely alone," Tom's familiar voice whispered gently. He reached out and drew me close to him, his strong arms wrapped around my body, his face buried in my hair, his lips hovering over my ear, kissing me tenderly. I could feel the pounding of his heart on my chest, and it was difficult to make out whose heart was beating at a faster pace. I tried, but was unable to bear the explosion of emotions inside me, and tears began to roll down my face.

In a quivering voice I whispered into Tom's ear, "I'm still in love with you."

Tom responded by tightening his embrace. Then he reached for my right hand, which was clutching his back. He pulled it gently toward his chest and placed it over his heart, with his hand firmly on mine. I could feel the racing of his heart against my palm.

I felt his warm breath in my ear. "I know, sweetheart, I know. It's okay."

Tom took my face into his hands and kissed me lovingly, his lips moving softly across my mouth. My lips immediately responded, and every inch of me focused on the feeling of Tom's body on mine. I wanted this moment to last forever. It felt like a dream, a dream I never wanted to wake from, and for the first time since returning to California, I felt like I had finally found my way home.

Chapter Sixteen

Come What May

A few days later, Tom approached me at the locker I shared with Liz. I had asked my fourth period teacher for a pass to collect an assignment that I had left inside my locker. When Tom appeared next to me, I was alone in the empty hallway near his classroom.

"Hi there," he said coyly.

"Hi," I replied while rummaging through my locker, "I left one of my assignments in here, and I need it for class."

"Lucky for me then."

I couldn't suppress a smile. "You realize we're standing right in front of the principal's office, right?"

"Yeah, I do. Since you mentioned Warren, you know what he said to me when he found out you were returning to Royal Oaks?"

"No, what did he say?"

"He said that he didn't want to see me within 50 feet of you, or else," Tom said matter-of-factly.

"What? Are you serious? Why didn't you tell me this before? Are you just *asking* to get caught?"

"Isabel," Tom said patiently, "Warren can't do anything to me. He's just trying to keep me on my toes. Anyway, as long as we're just talking, no one can accuse me of anything. Let's make this easier on both of us. Give me your new number and we can talk over the phone like we used to. That way you won't be so worried all the time, and I can stop constantly looking for you from my classroom and making excuses to come out and talk to you. We can both stop worrying about getting caught."

I nodded. "You're right, that would be better." I pulled a pen from my locker and started to jot my number on a piece of paper.

"No," Tom interrupted, putting a hand out. "Just tell me the number and I'll memorize it. I don't want anyone to see you hand me anything."

"Okay, but you'll remember it?"

"Isabel, anything about you becomes ingrained in my memory like carvings on stone."

Unable to control my blush, I rattled off my number. "You got that?"

He nodded. "I've committed it to memory." He scanned our surroundings out of the corner of his eye. "Is it okay if I call you tonight?"

"Sure," I said. "Call whenever you want, but make up a guy's name if my parents or my brother answer the phone. No more John, okay? My mom was giving me grief about blowing you off."

"Smart lady," Tom said with a smile on his face.

I closed my locker, assignment in hand. "I have to get going. I'll talk to you later?"

"Sure, Isabel, I'll call you tonight."

I skipped back to class, unable to contain my excitement. This seemed like exactly the solution we needed. We only wanted to talk, after all, and what was wrong with that?

As promised, Tom called me at home that evening just as I was heading into my bedroom after dinner.

"Isabel! Isabel, you have a phone call," my mother called from the kitchen.

I ran to the living room and grabbed the cordless phone from the cradle.

"Okay, thanks, Mami," I yelled back, rushing to my room. "You can hang up the kitchen phone now!"

I closed the door to my bedroom and held the receiver to my ear, waiting for the click of the other phone. When it came, I breathed out and cleared my throat.

"Hello?" I said, trying to sound casual.

"Hi there," the deep voice on the other end replied. "I'm glad I caught you. I've got about twenty minutes before Danielle gets home."

The mention of his wife's name immediately darkened my mood. Tom rarely talked about his wife, but on those occasions when he did, the harsh reality smothered my cheerful nature. *Nothing's going on, we're just talking*, I reminded myself. This was nothing like it had been before. I did my best to overcome my jealous mood, trying to focus on my conversation with Tom.

"Thanks for coming by my classroom the other day," he started, his voice dropping. "It was so good to feel you in my arms again. I'd forgotten how good you smell, how wonderful your lips felt. I didn't want to let you go."

"I know," I whispered back. "I wish I could've stayed in your arms forever. But we shouldn't be talking about that now."

There was a slight pause then he asked, "Do you have any plans for this Memorial Day weekend?"

"My uncle is visiting from Chile and my parents are taking him to Yosemite," I told him. "They leave on Friday morning, and I think they get back on Monday afternoon."

Tom laughed. "It's either coincidence or the stars are aligned in our favor. Danielle is taking the kids to Yosemite this weekend as well. She's going with friends of ours and their kids. They're leaving on Thursday morning and won't return until Monday night. I told her that I couldn't go - too many assignments to grade. It looks like we might have some time to spend together."

I sat up on my bed, pulling on a strand of my wet hair. The thought of spending time alone with Tom excited and frightened me at the same time. Was it crazy for us to pick up where we left off so quickly, despite the obvious risks? I was in love with him, and I knew that I wanted to be with him, but was it worth the danger? We were both putting ourselves at risk here, and for what?

"Tom, I –" I started, thinking that I should put an end to this before it started.

He paused expectantly, waiting for me to finish. When I didn't, he cleared his throat and spoke. "Yes, Isabel?"

I took a deep breath then spoke. "I just wonder if this is a good idea, that's all. There's so much at risk, and we –"

"Isabel, I can't live without you," he interrupted briskly. "I don't *want* to live without you. I love you, and I'm willing to risk anything to be with you. That's all there is to it." He paused for a second then continued. "Are you willing to take a risk with me, or is that too much for you?"

I gulped then nodded in agreement silently. That was the clearest he'd ever been on the subject, and it answered the questions I'd had. He was willing to risk everything for me. The least I could do, given how much we loved each other, was risk the same for him. "I would do anything to be with you," I murmured, putting my heart and soul behind the words.

"Good," he said, his voice softening. "Then that's settled. And maybe once we're alone, you can tell me why you stopped taking my calls last summer after I came back from my camping trip." His voice became serious again. "And why you didn't bother to say goodbye when you left to Chile. I thought you hated me, and it broke my heart."

"Tom, it wasn't anything you did," I told him. "Trust me. I was going through a lot before the move, and the emotions affected my thinking in all the wrong ways. I even wrote you a long letter from Chile explaining everything, but I never mailed it. I wrote it right before the police called me, and I figured it would be a terrible idea to mail it to you at school after you know, the incident. So I just tossed it out."

"The idea of not even saying goodbye to you drove me crazy," Tom said, a raw edge in his voice that both startled me and warmed my heart. "Anyway, we can talk about it later. So, let's plan on meeting up on Saturday, maybe in the late afternoon? How does that sound?"

"Sure," I replied. "It would be so nice to get to spend time alone again. And now that I have a car, it'll be easier for me. Where do you want to meet?"

There was a pause.

"To be honest, I would love it if you came over," Tom said. "It would be much more private for us here, instead of up in the mountains. What do you think?"

The idea of meeting him at his house – the home he shared with his wife and kids – sent a rush of blood to my brain and made me feel dizzy. I couldn't believe he was suggesting I meet him at his home. On top of that, though, there was the obvious fact of the danger involved.

"Do you really think that's a good idea?" I asked anxiously. "I mean, it's your home. What would your neighbors say if they saw me walking through your door while your wife is out of town?"

Tom chuckled. "Isabel, don't worry. Just come over. We'll sit around, cuddle for a few hours on the couch and catch up. That's it. You worry too much."

"Sorry, I can't help it." I took a deep breath and then said, "Fine. I'll come by your place on Saturday. Now you'd better get going."

"Goodnight, Isabel," Tom whispered.

"Goodnight," I replied softly. I hung up the phone and allowed a large, satisfied smile to form on my face.

"Wait a minute," Liz interrupted, lifting her hand up in the air with the flair of a pissed-off diva. "So, are you or aren't you?"

I was in Liz's bedroom, sitting on her large bed and cuddling with one of her oversized pillows. It was Saturday evening, and I'd just come from my rendezvous with Tom. There was something magical about being with an older man, something incredibly exhilarating and illicit. I'd found that everything was even more exciting when I told Liz about it, and I'd rushed straight here from his house. All of the worries, doubts, and guilt I harbored about being in a relationship with a married man fragmented and vanished when I talked to Liz about it. Besides that, talking to her made it feel real, rather than imaginary. If I was the only one who knew about it, then I could be imagining it all. If she knew as well, it made it real. I knew I shouldn't be talking to her, but I didn't want to stop.

I clenched the pillow in my hands and silenced my laughter with the feathery cloud. "What?" I slyly asked. "Can't you tell?"

Liz jumped on the bed and snatched the pillow from my hands. "Come on, Isabel, tell me! Are you still a virgin or not?"

"Well, it's difficult to say," I confessed. "We didn't actually have sex, but *something* certainly happened."

Liz looked as if she was going to burst with anticipation.

"I want to hear everything, from the start," she demanded. "What did you guys do? Were you on his bed? Tell me everything, from the beginning!"

"All right." I took a moment to organize the details of the afternoon in my head. "I parked about a block away from his place because I didn't want his neighbors to see an unfamiliar car outside his house. I walked to up the porch and knocked on the front door. Within a few seconds, he came to let me in. He walked me straight to the sofa in the living room, but before we started anything, he told me something that I still don't believe … well, I don't know, maybe it's true…"

"What, Isabel? What did he say?"

"Well, you know how I'm freaked out about losing my virginity to just any guy, and how I don't want to have sex because I'm terrified of getting pregnant and my parents killing me?"

"Yeah, so what? Who isn't?"

"Apparently, Tom decided to get a vasectomy a few weeks ago. I mean, he said he told his wife it was because he didn't want to have any more kids, but he said he did it because of me."

Liz began to laugh. "Are you kidding me? What does that mean?"

"He said he didn't want me to worry so much. I had told him that I didn't want to sleep with him until I was ready, and until I knew that it would be safe ... you know, until I knew that I wouldn't get pregnant. Well, I think he took that seriously. Anyway, maybe he's just saying that, maybe the truth is his wife forced him to get one so that she wouldn't get pregnant again. You know, guys can say all kinds of things to have sex and it's impossible to know exactly what's true and what isn't. I think he really got one, you know, got the surgery, but I don't know why he really did it. Anyway, who cares? That's not really important."

"Okay, fine. Come on, get to the good stuff," Liz said impatiently.

"Then Tom excused himself for a minute, so I took the opportunity to look around. His house was nice. It was pretty small, but cozy. The first thing I looked for were pictures of him and his wife, or his kids. Can you believe there was nothing?"

"Maybe he took them down because he knew they would make you feel uncomfortable," Liz answered. "Or maybe they just don't keep pictures up."

"I thought there would be pictures for sure. After all, Tom's a photography teacher! Well, maybe you're right, maybe he took them down for my sake. I obviously wasn't going to ask him why there were no pictures. Anyway, Tom came back and we sat on the sofa together. It was kind of weird being there, in complete privacy. Most times I'm thinking about who might drive up and see us naked in the truck, or who might open the door when we're in his classroom, or who's going to pick up the phone when we're talking. This time it was like we were completely free. Okay, actually, I was afraid that his wife might have forgotten something at home and come back to find us on the couch."

Liz giggled. "That would've completely sucked! I'm sure Tom was worrying about the same thing."

"Actually, he seemed pretty relaxed," I told her. "It's almost unsettling how easygoing he is about the whole thing, like it doesn't really phase him. I'm not sure what to make of it. But then again, he's a very easy going and relaxed guy. That's his personality, after all. Anyway, he sat on the sofa and seemed really comfortable holding me in his arms. We talked for a while, about everything that's happened, and then we started making out. First we were kissing, just sitting up on the sofa, then before I knew it, we were lying naked on the sofa, tossing and turning…"

"What do you mean tossing and turning? Was he on top or were you? Come on, you're flying past the details, Isabel!"

I paused, thinking back to the events of the afternoon. I knew that I was leaving things out and telling her only half the story, but a large part of me didn't want to tell her everything. That part of me wanted to keep it a secret, to keep those special moments between Tom and me private, to be shared between the two of us. "Listen, Liz, we did a lot of stuff, and it all felt incredible. But this was our first time, really, and I don't want to give up *all* the details. I want to keep some to myself, you know?" I looked up at her, hoping that she'd understand.

Liz's bright eyes dimmed a bit, and her face fell. "Yeah, I understand," she said slowly. "It's probably not a good idea for you to tell me everything, anyhow. You know, in case the police decide to torture me for information!" She shrieked with laughter and threw a pillow at me. "I can't believe you guys finally did something more than just make out!"

I shook my head somberly. "Well it didn't go much farther than that, to be honest. We tried to … you know … but it didn't work. He finally stopped, and told me that he didn't think I was ready. You can't believe how frustrated and embarrassed I felt, Liz. I mean, mentally and emotionally I was there, I wanted it, I wanted him to be the *one*, you know, but my body was just rejecting him. I swear I never thought it would be so difficult to have sex. Anyway, I told him to keep trying, I even said it didn't hurt that much, but I think he saw right through me because after a few more attempts, he stopped and just held me in his arms. He was really sweet about it. He told me that he wanted me to be ready, and we would try again some other time, but he didn't want to hurt me."

"That's it?" Liz asked, disappointed.

I shrugged. "Yep. We got dressed and I told him I had to get home. I was so embarrassed, and I just wanted to leave. He wanted to cuddle with me, kiss me, and hold me in his arms, but I was so upset with myself that I just wanted to go. It was like my body had let me down."

Liz frowned. "Isabel, don't be so hard on yourself. Don't worry. I bet next time it will be much easier. Remember how much I told you it hurt the first time Brad and I had sex? How we had to keep trying? Next time it will happen, you'll see. Now tell me, when are you going back?"

"He asked me to spend the night tomorrow," I replied. "It's our only opportunity to spend the night together, since my parents and his wife come back on Monday. I want to try again. Liz, I'm completely in love with him, and I know I don't want to lose my virginity to anyone else. I just hope it hurts a little less next time."

"Don't worry, Isabel. You have to concentrate on relaxing, okay? When you're with him tomorrow night, you just need to relax your whole body and just let go. It'll hurt less."

"I'll just tell my brother that I'm spending the night here at your house," I told her. "He won't care, he's so busy these days. But just in case he calls, which he won't, just make sure you answer the phone and tell him that I'm in the shower or something."

"Sure thing," Liz replied. She grabbed a hold of my hands and looked at me earnestly. "Look, tomorrow it'll happen. Don't worry about it - you just have to relax and let your mind and body go."

Tomorrow would be my night; I was sure of it, and I was prepared to do whatever I could to make the night not only pleasurable but memorable as well.

Chapter Seventeen

No Ordinary Love

*S*unday afternoon dragged on endlessly. The spring days were drawn out and the sun didn't set until well past 8 o'clock in the evening. I began nursing a glass of red wine from the open bottle that my parents had left on the kitchen counter. She would hardly notice if the bottle were slightly emptier than before. As a Chilean, I was raised with wine on the dinner table, and I'd started drinking the beverage during holidays or family gatherings when I was fourteen. I enjoyed the soft, tart drink for the warmth it brought to my body, and I thought it would help me relax.

I finished the generous glass and switched to water, then went to sit on the couch. I had on my most comfortable clothes – gray sweats and an old t-shirt – and felt more relaxed than I had in weeks. It was nearly time for Tom to call and let me know that it was safe to drive to his house, and I was ready for the night to begin.

I snatched the phone up immediately when it rang. "Hello?"

"Are you busy?" came a deep voice on the other end of the line.

"Not really," I said with a broad grin on my face. "Did you have any plans?"

"Actually, I thought maybe you could come over and spend the night," Tom said playfully. "What do you think?"

Tom always enjoyed playing these little games with me. Instead of saying "All right, it's all clear, you can come over now," he acted as if we hadn't planned this whole thing out. He loved the idea that we were playing things by ear, and being spontaneous.

"Mmm, good idea," I whispered softly into the phone. "I think I'm up for that. But I must warn you, I'm in my sweats and a t-shirt."

"Sweetheart, just come as you are."

"All right, I can be there in ten minutes."

When I hung up the phone and stood up, my head began to spin a little. I realized that if I wanted to make it to Tom's house safely, I had to at least sober up a little first. I walked to the kitchen for a second glass of water, brushed my teeth, sprayed on some perfume, combed my hair, and put some Vaseline on my lips. By the time I was done, I was feeling confident enough to drive the few miles across town. I grabbed my keys, made sure all of the doors were locked, and walked toward my car.

I made it to Tom's house without any mishaps, and parked directly across the street this time. When I reached Tom's front door, I saw that the house was completely dark except for the porch light. I knocked softly and waited. The night air was breezy, but warm, and I could just make out the scent of star jasmine.

As I waited, I reconsidered my attire. *Sweats?* I thought. *What's wrong with me?* The women in romance novels didn't seduce their men wearing sweatpants and t-shirts! I hadn't been paying attention when I left the house, and even if I had been, I couldn't show up at a married man's door dressed in nothing but a robe or wearing sexy Victoria's Secret lingerie. Sweats were appropriate, I assured myself, and would throw off any suspicion. Although I was still concerned a prying neighbor would see me at his doorstep, I tried not to worry and focus on what would happen when I walked through the door.

The door creaked open and Tom stood in the dim light of what appeared to be flickering candles inside. He extended his hand toward me.

"Come on, Isabel, before anyone sees you," he muttered.

Tom led me into the dimly lit living room, holding my hand. The smell of his freshly washed hair reminded me of the first time we had hugged, and I shivered. He looked at me anxiously then smiled.

"Are you ready for bed?"

"Of course," I whispered, hoping I had brushed my teeth well enough to camouflage the scent of wine on my breath.

Tom nodded and led me toward the stairs. I was surprised; I had thought we would end up on the living room sofa again. I tried to imagine sleeping with Tom in the bed he shared with his wife, and failed. I was surprised that he seemed comfortable with the idea.

When we finally made it to the top of the carpeted staircase, a flickering light coming from the open bedroom door illuminated the small hallway. More candles, I thought. To my left was a door with two colorful wooden nameplates hanging from two white nails: Nell and Erin. His daughters' shared bedroom. I looked away, feeling the first inkling of guilt.

Tom led me into his bedroom, and I looked quickly around. The candle on top of the chest of drawers directly in front of the bed was the only source of light in the entire room. There were no picture frames, mementos, or even paintings on the walls. Had Tom taken everything down? Above the bed, a rectangular window sat in the wall, covered with a white fabric curtain. The curtain was only partially drawn, allowing a stream of soft light to filter through. The moonlight cloaked the bed with a subtle, romantic glow.

"I'm so glad you're here, Isabel," Tom whispered. He took my hands in his and motioned me to sit next to him. I said nothing, and he moved to stroke my hair softly. "I don't know what happened in Chile, but I'm so happy you're back here, back in my arms."

"I don't really want to talk about Chile," I said, not meeting his eyes. The rumpled sheet felt cool under the palm of my hand and the carpeted floor still had faint vacuum marks on it. "What I need you to know is that I was careless with my friends and that's how the police got involved … but I never, ever meant for anything bad to happen to you. I'm so sorry about what you had to go through."

Tom inched his way toward me; our bodies met softly and with purpose, and within seconds, we were lying comfortably side-by-side on the mattress. Tom's lips tasted mine as if for the first time and his tongue was warm and fluid in my mouth; I could feel it twirl around mine softly. He moved from my lips to my neck, and when it was time to remove my t-shirt, he stopped.

"Isabel, are you sure you're ready?" he asked. "I mean, are you really sure you want to do this? I need to know that you don't feel pressured and this is something you really want to do."

"There's nothing I want more," I assured him. "I'm very ready for this. I want it to be with you. There's no pressure here, I'm doing this because it's what I want."

My words were enough. I lost track of time as Tom traced my body with his mouth and gentle touch. He spent nearly half of the time making love to me with his moist lips and wet tongue. I welcomed his body on mine, to do what it pleased.

After what seemed like forever, Tom sat up in bed and reached for the small drawer on the nightstand. My eyes followed his movement as he took out a white tube. He unscrewed the small cap and squeezed a small amount of the transparent gel onto his forefinger.

"This is a lubricant," Tom said; he recapped the tube and placed it back in the nightstand where it belonged, and then he resumed his position next to me in bed. He took his forefinger and rubbed the gel gently *there*. "Hopefully it'll ease your pain a little bit. The last thing I want is to hurt you."

"Look, no matter what, my first time is going to hurt," I told him. "I've just got to get past that. I just ask that you're gentle. After the first time, it should be fine. So for now, don't worry about me. If it's too much for me to handle, I'll let you know."

Tom began to kiss me again, first tenderly and then passionately. After a few minutes of intense kissing, I could feel Tom's stiffness rubbing up against me, now slippery with gel. The slight pressure of his sex against my skin was driving me crazy, and he continued to tease me until I could no longer control myself. I wanted, I needed to feel him inside of me or I would burst with desire. Tom's body began thrusting gently into mine. Although I still felt a reminiscent sting, the pain was much less severe. My insides still convulsed and attempted to expel the intrusion, but each gentle thrust brought with it a titillating feeling that gradually overcame the pain I felt.

I moved with Tom, feeling him inch inward with every thrust, and the pressure I felt, similar to what I had felt yesterday afternoon, increased. Then I felt my insides tear open, as if from one end to the other, and the pressure was replaced with a burning feeling as Tom made his way deeper and deeper into me. The pain overwhelmed me and I bit down on my lip to stop from screaming out in pain. I suffered in silence; I would have to feel this pain to finally feel pleasure, so it was now or never.

"Isabel, are you okay?" Tom asked as he eased his movement. "Should I stop? Does it hurt too much?"

"I'm fine," I gasped. In spite of my pain, I wanted him to finally orgasm so my body could take a break and begin to heal itself. "Don't stop, just keep going."

Calling out my name, Tom climaxed; although my body was exhausted from the pain of being ripped open for the first time, I reveled in the feeling of Tom's first orgasm with me. A warm emotion rushed through my body and although I was nowhere near reaching a physical orgasm, I felt an emotional climax that was unlike anything I had ever experienced before.

I held onto Tom lovingly as he lay on top of me, kissing my neck tenderly and caressing my hair. At that precise moment, I wanted to hold on to this man forever. I wanted never to let him go, to lie like this for eternity. This was the closest and most intimate moment I had ever spent with another human being and although the pain was indescribable, I was in a state of absolute bliss.

Chapter Eighteen

Sweet Surrender

The break of dawn ushered in a lovely pale yellow glow, which woke me from a peaceful slumber. Could it have all been a dream? My body felt heavy but at peace and I realized that Tom was resting against me, snuggling at my side. I could hardly believe it; here I was, lying in a matrimonial bed with a married man, enjoying the afterglow of losing my virginity to the man I loved. I held on to Tom's warm body and relished the moment, knowing that we'd have to part ways soon. My fingers twirled around his dirty blonde locks, waking him from sleep.

"What time is it?" he whispered, half asleep. "Are we late for school?"

Glancing at the antique clock on the wall next to the bed, I replied, "It's only five thirty, so we still have some time."

Tom took a firm hold of me again. "Isabel, I wish we could stay like this forever. I want to hold you in my arms every night until the day I die."

He began to kiss me passionately; our bodies rolled from one side of the bed to the other and before I knew it, we were making love for a second time. My semi-experienced body seemed to respond more positively to Tom, and with each thrust, I felt less pain and more pleasure. The lovemaking was still not pain-free, but somehow my body sensed something new, something exciting that it had not previously experienced. It felt as though a dormant sensor had been set off and within a few moments the sensor sent out an alarm, which pulsated throughout my body. Tom continued to thrust, deeper and quicker until I could hardly take it anymore. Is this what Liz meant when she said that sex felt *unbearably* good?

As Tom climaxed, I felt a pure sense of satisfaction because, not only did Tom find making love with me pleasurable, but I also finally allowed myself to let go and *feel*. I was convinced that during future lovemaking sessions, Tom would satisfy me the way no other man could.

He rested on top of me afterwards, kissing me tenderly, his lips caressing mine. I was warm with love and affection and felt a genuine, deep connection between the two of us. Tom and I were merged into one; in a sense, we were one. As soon as he shifted his weight off of me and rolled over to get out of bed, an instant feeling of separation and melancholy took hold of me. It was time to part ways, and time for me to go home. Mine was an impossible love, and could only exist if hidden from society's judgmental eye, just like in a Johanna Lindsey romance novel.

Once we were out of bed and fully dressed again – me in my sweatpants and t-shirt, Tom in his jeans and dark gray polo shirt – he took me in his arms to say goodbye. We stood together, readying ourselves to face the world outside, and I nestled my face against Tom's chest.

"Are you okay, sweetheart?" Tom whispered in my ear.

The way he asked about my wellbeing made me blush and drove home the fact that he wholeheartedly cared about me. Trying to conceal my sleepy voice, I said, "Yeah, I'm good. Just a bit sore, but it was worth it."

Tom chuckled. "Was this *really* your first time?"

I pulled back, feeling offended. "Are you kidding me? Really? You think I would just *say* I'm a virgin? Why would I do that? Did it feel like I was a virgin to you? I mean, the only reason I didn't cry out in pain was because I didn't want to discourage you from finishing."

"Isabel, I'm not saying you lied to me," Tom said quickly. "I just find it so hard to believe that someone as sexy and confident as you can still be a virgin. There must be a line of guys waiting to have a chance with you, and you picked me to be the first one? Don't get me wrong, I'm completely honored. I hope you were comfortable because I was trying to be as gentle as possible."

"If you weren't one hundred percent sure I was a virgin, then why would you make love to me without any protection?" I demanded, feeling betrayed and confused. "So you had a vasectomy, that just ensures that I don't get pregnant; but what about STDs like AIDS? Weren't you worried about that?" I gasped, suddenly realizing that I should have been worried about that as well. I didn't know much about STDs, but I knew how easily they could go around, and who knew what his wife did when he wasn't home? Did he trust her to be faithful? Did I trust her to be faithful? Had my naïve trust just put me in danger? I looked at Tom again, afraid of what else I had done to put myself at risk, and pouted.

Tom reached out and held me still so that he could look straight into my eyes, "Isabel, I trust you. I'm sure you know that lots of girls trick guys about their virginity. But you know what? I believe you, Isabel. All I've been doing ever since I met you is taking risks. I'm risking my family, my career … I'm putting everything on the line for you. Last night could have been a huge risk, for both of us really, but it won't be because we trust each other. You do trust me too, right, Isabel? You believe that I got a vasectomy, don't you? You believe that I'll keep you safe?"

As always, I softened under Tom's hypnotic spell. He knew what to say and when to say it. I couldn't help but smile, and my shoulders relaxed.

"Yes, I do," I replied. "You would be really stupid if you lied to me about that, because I'm sure the last thing you need is for a sixteen-year-old to be pregnant with your baby. I do trust you."

Tom took me in his arms and whispered in my ear, "Isabel, I don't know how I could possibly love you more than I do right now."

I leaned up and kissed Tom's neck. "You don't know how much I wish I could be the one you fall asleep with every night. I love you with all my heart, Tom."

Tom and I kissed goodbye inside his doorway, and then he quickly escorted me to my car. He seemed to be walking with intent as he strode across the street. I noticed him snatch something from my under the wipers of my windshield and stash it quickly in his pocket.

"What was that? What did you put in your pocket?" I asked nervously.

"Nothing, Isabel, don't worry," he said hurriedly. "It's just a parking ticket. It's illegal to leave cars parked overnight on the street in this neighborhood. Don't worry, I'll take care of it."

"Why didn't you tell me? I would have parked somewhere else," I replied. "Just give me the ticket. I can pay for it. Please? Can you give me that ticket? There's no reason for you to pay for it."

"Isabel, you're not paying for anything," Tom said firmly. "Now, drive carefully, okay? I love you."

"I love you, too."

I got in my car, keeping my eye on Tom in my rearview mirror. He disappeared into his house, glancing back toward my car, a satisfied smile on his face.

Chapter Nineteen

Into Temptation

"Morning, Isabel. How are we today?" James asked as I walked through the main department store doors ten minutes late. After leaving Tom's house, I had tried my very best to be quick while getting ready, but I lingered in the shower, allowing the hot water to flow through my broken flesh. I was incredibly tired and felt as though I had not gotten a wink of sleep the entire night.

When I walked into the department store I felt self-conscious, almost as if every person in that place would somehow know that I was no longer a virgin, that something was completely different about me. Could guys tell these things just by looking at a girl?

"Hi James. I'm fine," I replied in a tired, quiet voice. "Should I go straight down to the warehouse? Where do you want me?"

"Walk with me, Isabel," James said as he placed his hand on the small of my back ushering me slightly forward. "Let's go to the women's department so you can help me arrange the new shipment of clothes."

We walked, James and I, side by side down the newly shined marble walkway toward the end of the department store where the women's department was located. Every step I took reminded me of the night with Tom; my insides still raw. When we finally made it to the floor where we would be working, I noticed that we were the only ones around. "James? Where's everyone else? Isn't anyone going to help us?"

James had already begun arranging the clothes on the display racks, his strong hands taking ten to fifteen dresses from the warehouse cart to the display rack at one time. His muscles rippled under his perfectly fitted white polo shirt and his legs moved with purpose under his snug-fitting dark blue jeans that framed his bottom ever so nicely. "I've got everyone else down in the warehouse because a shipment arrived last night. They'll be working there all morning. Why? You want me to switch you out with someone else?" James asked without looking up at me from his work.

"No, I was just wondering where everyone was, that's all."

James stood tall with a handful of petit black cocktail dresses, as he held them neatly in his hand; he looked straight into my eyes and said, "out of everyone who works here, I'd rather have you helping me out. It gives me the opportunity to pick your brain and get to know you a little better. Anyway, this is a lighter job, I thought maybe you would appreciate it."

"You're sweet James, thanks," I replied sluggishly, as I continued to help with the cocktail dresses, taking two at a time from cart to shiny metallic display rack. "I do appreciate it because I'm tired and the last thing I want to do this morning is work the warehouse."

James picked up the pace using both hands to grab what seemed like twenty-five dresses at a time. As he worked, he continued to be inquisitive, asking general questions but also getting personal from time to time. After about an hour of hanging clothes and arranging display racks, my shift was over and it was time to clock out and head to school for third period. "It's time for you to call it quits, Isabel. I'll clock you out later. Come on, let me walk you to your car." James pushed the dingy warehouse carts to the corner of the floor and began to walk with me at his side.

"James, are you sure?" I asked. "I can clock out and rush to school for class. No need for you to walk me to my car."

"Are you trying to get rid of me? I just want to talk to you for a minute outside, is that alright?" James asked with a slightly concerned look on his face.

Somewhat hesitant, I responded, "Okay, that's fine, but I'm in a hurry."

As soon as we got to my car, parked near the entrance of the department store, James opened the car door for me. I could feel the warm air pushing my loose hair away from my face. I stood there wondering what it was he wanted to say to me. As soon as I sat in the driver's seat, James took a piece of paper out of his pocket and casually handed it to me. "This is my number, Isabel, use it when you like. I didn't want to give it to you inside because I know how all those high school kids gossip in there. Your training ends in about two weeks, so I wanted to make sure that we stay in contact even after you stop coming here in the mornings. Why don't you write down your number for me and I'll call you?" He asked, batting his thick lashes shyly.

In an effort to expedite the uncomfortable moment with my supervisor, I ripped a small section of the paper he had just handed me and wrote down my phone number. I handed the tiny white paper to him, "Here you go, James. Now, I should really get going because I'm going to be late for class."

James carefully closed the door and I turned on the ignition. He placed one hand on my door, window rolled down, and looked me square in the eye, "I'll call you, Isabel, and then maybe we can meet up somewhere and hang out." He was so close I could smell the scent of his *Aqua de Gio* cologne. It smelled so clean and masculine, yet so subtle - it drove me crazy.

"Okay, whenever you like. See you tomorrow, James," I said cheerfully and then drove off to class.

"Isabel! You've got a phone call!" my mom shouted from her office.

Sitting comfortably on the leather sofa watching T.V., I shouted back at the top of my lungs, "Who is it, Mami?"

"Someone named James! Can you just pick up the phone, please? I'm very busy here and I don't have time to be your secretary!" my mom shouted back, somewhat annoyed at my lethargy.

Upon hearing the name *James* resonate from my mom's office, I was instantly motivated to get off the sofa and reach for the cordless phone on the corner table just feet away from where I was lounging.

"Hello?"

A timid, yet deep voice responded, "Hi Isabel? How are you?"

"I'm fine, just watching T.V. What's up with you?"

James cleared his throat, "Well, I just thought since retail training ended last week, officially, maybe it was okay for us to talk."

"James, aren't you getting married two weeks or something?" I jokingly reminded him.

I could hear James chuckle under his breath. "Yeah, my wedding is two weeks from Saturday which is why I wanted to see if we could meet up *before* then. It's just that I think you're a really cool girl. I just want to spend some time with you before I no longer have that opportunity. Would you be up for that?"

The fact that James was pursuing me was exhilarating because every girl in my retail-training class was absolutely in lust with the guy. Somehow I had sparked his interest and although Tom was the sole owner of my heart, I was not about to allow this opportunity to slip past me. After all, I was a sixteen-year-old girl with recently discovered feminine wiles.

"Yeah, sure. We could meet up if you like. What do you propose?"

A few seconds passed as James hemmed and hawed uncomfortably, "Well, I really don't know. I hadn't thought about where we could meet. Do you have any ideas?"

Without giving it a second thought, I blurted, "What if we meet tomorrow afternoon. Class ends at three and I'll be attending graduation at six, since a lot of my senior friends are graduating tomorrow. Why don't we meet at three thirty for a little while up in the mountains?"

"The mountains?" James asked, "What do you mean? What mountains?"

"My friends and I usually hang out and drink up there. It's pretty private, so why don't we meet down at the foothills and drive up together?" How could such words escape from my mouth? I thought to myself. Had I gone mad?

"Okay, that's cool," he replied confidently, "just tell me where to meet you and I'll be there."

Although I felt a twinge of remorse over proposing the sacred location where Tom and I shared our most intimate moments together, I was in no position to back peddle. So, I gave James directions.

"Ok Isabel, I know exactly where that is. You better not bail on me," James said sarcastically.

Hoping to bring the conversation to a close because my dad had walked unexpectedly through the living room where I was sitting, I said, "Don't worry, I'll be there. Now, I have to run. I'll see you tomorrow, okay?"

"Okay, sweet dreams, Isabel."

"Thanks, you too. Goodnight."

I could not forge a single moment of slumber when my head hit the pillow that night. Over and over again, I tortured myself for having offered such a sacred location for my meeting with James. If Tom were to find out about what I had agreed to, about what I was planning to do with someone else, his heart would be broken. How could I have done such a thing? Was there nowhere else I could have met James? The more important question I didn't ask myself was: why did I agree to meet up with an engaged guy anyway? Was my illicit affair with a married teacher who was twice my age not enough to keep me busy?

During that sleepless night, all I thought about was my impending meeting with James and my lack of loyalty to Tom. I began to feel a great sense of despair, and I wanted to back out of meeting James because it could lead to nothing but more carelessness on my part. Guilt engulfed me and nearly twenty hours before committing what felt like adultery, I felt horrible for what might take place between James and myself. My concern was not with James' fiancé; rather, I felt a huge weight on my shoulders at the possibility of being unfaithful to Tom. This would not be a trivial rendezvous like the one I had with Ryan in Europe; things were much different now. Tom and

I were in a serious, adult relationship; we were making love regularly and above all, we were committed to each other. Yet, at that moment, lying sleepless in my twin sized bed and tormented by my imminent infidelity, something clear and obvious hit me like a ton of bricks: Tom was sleeping with another woman in the bed where I had lost my virginity! In effect, he was being unfaithful, not just to his wife for harboring a secret, but he was also being unfaithful to *me* by being with his wife. Tom never appeared to be beleaguered by the fact that I was being cheated on every time he laid to rest with his wife, so why should I torment myself because I intended on possibly kissing another guy? The circumstances were unjust. Did Tom cease making love to his wife because he was making love with me? Of course not! The thought of Tom making love to another woman distressed me enough that I convinced myself it was absolutely okay to go forward with James. I did not necessarily have to feel good about what I might do with him, but there was no logical reason for me to feel guilty. My intention was never to hurt Tom, but I wanted him to feel the jealousy and pain I experienced every day.

James was already parked in the dusty parking lot when I arrived. Tom had delayed me by lingering at my locker making small talk. He wanted to be sure he would see me at graduation later that evening and above all, he wanted to know if I would have an extra thirty minutes after graduation to spend with him. Unfortunately, I had to turn Tom down because I had already made plans to hang with Liz after graduation and spend the night at her house. Tom was disappointed but assured me that seeing me at graduation would be enough to get him through the weekend.

In my denim short shorts and a cream colored, fitted v-cut tank top, which just barely revealed my developing cleavage to anyone who stood taller than me, I walked casually from my car to James' small black sports car. James was nothing like Tom, and he did not exhibit Tom's patience either. Rather than waiting for me in his car, I saw James pacing around his sports car as I drove up to the empty lot. Recognizing my car, he stopped and waited for me to park and walk over to where he was. In fitted jeans, which embellished his perfectly shaped behind that he was famous for, he resembled a Roman warrior, strong and proud. James always seemed to stand with purpose, and today was no different.

"Hi there," I smiled as I walked up to him.

James looked at me and smiled, exposing his perfectly straight and ultra-white teeth. "Well, are you ready to drive up, Isabel?"

"Okay, do you want to drive or should I?"

James walked over to his car's passenger door and opened it for me, waiting until I was comfortably seated inside the sporty leather bucket seat to close the door. As James made his way from my door to his, I inadvertently wondered when his fiancé had last sat in this seat. Had he just dropped her off at home and then driven here to meet me? My thoughts quickly jumped from James' fiancé to Tom. What if Tom drove by and saw my car parked at the base of the mountains? What would he think? What would he say? I should have offered to drive up. Tom lived just minutes away from this mountain road, and it was possible for him to drive home and pass by the parking lot, wasn't it? If that were to occur, Tom would recognize my car and put two and two together. The mere idea of Tom finding out I was in our sacred mountain retreat with another guy made my skin crawl and instantly, I felt as white as a ghost.

James interrupted my thoughts abruptly, "Hey, Isabel, did you hear about O.J. Simpson today?"

I was in a confused state of neither here nor there. "I don't know," I answered indifferently, "What are you talking about?"

James continued to drive up the winding road; he drove harshly and quickly as if time were of the essence. Glancing at me from time to time, he continued, "O.J. Simpson. It was all over the news today. O.J.'s ex-wife and her friend were murdered last night in Brentwood. Apparently, the cops think O.J. murdered them in a rage. It's insane!"

I didn't understand the significance of these events, "Who's O.J. Simpson?" I asked innocently.

James looked at me incredulously as he made an abrupt, tight turn, "Are you kidding me? You don't know who O.J. is? He's a football legend."

"Oh, I don't follow sports," feeling vindicated, I continued, "although, I know all the famous football players, like Pelé and Maradona."

"No, not soccer. I'm talking about American football. O.J. was a famous football player. He's a millionaire," James stressed.

Still unmoved by the news, I said, "Oh, okay. So it's a big deal that he killed his ex-wife and her friend. I guess that makes sense. I've been at school, so I haven't heard about it yet."

"Well, it's going to be a huge case, I'm sure of it. O.J.'s pretty important in the sports world and his wife comes from a well-to-do family, so they're not going to rest until O.J. hangs for the murders."

Playing devil's advocate, I had to ask, "Maybe he didn't do it. You know, cops are notorious for framing minorities, especially in L.A."

James and I continued to engage in small talk for about twenty minutes, until he finally pointed to a look-out-point, "So, Isabel, do you think we should park over there? I don't want to drive forever because I know you have to get going in an hour or so."

I nodded my head in affirmation, "Sure, we can stop there." I breathed a sigh of relief when I realized that we had passed the small dirt road that led to the shady green spot where Tom and I would park for hours and enjoy our intimate love making sessions. James had pulled up to a traditional look-out-point, which was very exposed. I opened my door first, and James followed. We walked at a distance from each other toward the edge of the look-out-point. James and I stood at the edge, looking down toward the hazy valley that rested below. We were both silent and I could only guess that he was as nervous as I was. The green leaves of the trees nearby were rustling with the gentle, warm breeze that was blowing. The scent of soil and vegetation reminded me of Tom, of our time spent together in these mountains. What was I doing up here with this guy? I asked myself. It was still unclear to me what would happen next, and sensing the awkwardness of the moment, I asked, "What time is it, James?"

Rather than verbalize the time, James raised his bare arm to show me the time on his wristwatch. As if possessed by an unfamiliar aggressive instinct, I took his wrist in my hand and looked up at him. The look I gave him must have communicated, "kiss me right now!" because James' lips came crashing down on mine. My mind was spinning as I felt his tongue clumsily searching for mine. Was this really happening? Was I really standing over this precipice in the arms of this guy, who was my former supervisor and also very much engaged? The senses that rushed through my body confirmed that these unbelievable events were actually unfolding. James was kissing me passionately, but awkwardly. His tongue felt small and inept in my mouth; his lips were firm and tight, not soft and relaxed as Tom's were; and his hands were searching the curves of my body tensely. It was immediately clear to me that I was not enjoying the moment with James; in fact, I wanted the kissing and the groping to cease at once. My lips did not conform to his, but rather were repelled; my tongue did not move in tandem with his, it made every attempt to deter the incursion; and my hands did not involuntarily explore his body with tenderness; instead, they remained limp and life-less at my sides.

James must have noticed my general lack of interest because after his attempt at a prolonged kiss, he slowly pulled away and looked down at the valley below.

I wanted to flee the situation as soon as possible. "We should get going, James. I've still got to get home and shower before graduation tonight. I don't want to be late because I've got a lot of close friends graduating and chances are, I won't see them again after tonight."

"I thought you were just a junior?" James asked, perplexed by my insistence on arriving at graduation on time.

"I'm not graduating tonight, I *am* a junior, but I have friends that are seniors and I want to see them graduate."

James didn't reply, he simply walked back to his car and turned on the ignition. I quickly followed and sat in the passenger seat next to him. I'll never know if James' ego was bruised or if he was just sulking because he wanted to spend more time with me, but from the moment we got into his car to the moment he dropped me off at the parking lot, words were not exchanged. Instead, James turned up the radio and listened to the news unfolding about the O.J. case, which I was completely disinterested in. At the base of the mountain, I hastily moved to open the door to get out of James' car as fast as possible. He grabbed my left arm brutishly, however, and said, "Don't I get a goodbye kiss?"

If that was the only way to flee the scene quickly, then so be it. Before getting out of the car, I reached over and forced a smile, then rested my lips lightly on his. James was not satisfied with the light peck so he firmly gripped the back of my head with his left hand and forced my mouth open with his commanding tongue. I feverishly whipped my tongue around in his mouth for a moment and then struggled to get free.

"I have to go. See you later," I said in haste jumping out of his car.

Fortunately for me, James didn't get out of his car; he simply waited for me to get into my car. He rolled down his passenger window and shouted out, "Bye, Isabel! I'll call you later."

James was true to his promise. During the two weeks that led up to his wedding day, he called my house nearly every day, but I had diligently protected myself from James by telling my mom that I was not answering any of his phone calls. To my delight, it was no coincidence that James' incessant phone calls ceased following his wedding day.

Chapter Twenty

Just Like Heaven

Soon Tom and I were back to our normal schedule. We met at the coffee shop down the road, or the local library, or the market on the corner, and drove to the mountains together. I fell more and more in love with him, and found ways to push away the guilt and concern over the situation. I also found a way to believe that Tom and his wife were just roommates, as he had alluded to on several occasions.

"I don't even love her anymore, to be honest," he told me as we drove up the mountain. "I wish she would divorce me, but I've asked and she's refused. I don't know what to do about it. If it weren't for the girls, I would just leave."

I nodded, trying not to think about the fact that he had a wife and kids at home. We tried not to talk about them, since they brought our moods down, but Liz asked about them fairly often. If he loved me so much, and wanted me so badly, why was he still with her? Why did they still sleep in the same bed? Why was he working so hard to keep her in the dark about his true feelings?

"Don't you think it would be better for you if you talked to her about it?" I asked quietly. "I mean, tell her that you don't love her anymore. Surely she doesn't want to stay in a marriage that's devoid of love?"

Tom reached a convenient parking place and turned off the engine, turning to me. "Are you complaining?" he asked quietly. "You're not satisfied with the way things are? You know we could never be together, Isabel, even if I wasn't married. Not until you turn eighteen, and even then it would be frowned upon. Being married gives me a convenient cover, surely you can see that. It means that other people suspect me less." He paused and gave me one of his charming grins. "I'm happily married, with two kids. Why on earth would I be involved with a student?"

I faked a smile, knowing that he was trying to make me feel better, but something in my heart cracked. He was joking, I thought, though there was too much truth in the joke for it to be truly funny. His joke was too close to reality and I found nothing entertaining about it.

"Danielle isn't responsive or affectionate. It's just totally different … she's like my roommate. Isabel, it has always been you. There has never been anyone else, you know that," Tom said quietly as he parked under the canopy in our secret spot off the main winding mountain road. I nodded, praying that he was telling me the truth, and allowed him to pull me onto his lap. Before long, I forgot to think at all.

Junior year came to an end, and I breathed a sigh of relief at the onset of summer. This gave me more time to spend with Tom, and less time in the public eye. One late June afternoon, though, my mom confronted me in the driveway. I was on my way back from Tom's house, and had spotted her in the front yard from a block away, so she didn't surprise me. What she had, though, spelled an end to my pleasant reverie.

She was holding a stack of envelopes in her hand and stormed toward the car, shouting at me to get out of the car. She glared down at me, her chest heaving under her perfectly tailored business coat. "What is your problem? Do you have no sense of responsibility?"

"What is it, Ma? What are you talking about?" I asked, glancing at the envelopes in her hand. What had she found? Had I been careless and left some of the letters out? My eyes jumped back up to her face, afraid of what I might see there.

My mother waved an envelope in my face. "Were you not going to say anything about this parking ticket, Isabel? Did you think it would just go away? Tell me, when and where did you get this ticket?"

The parking ticket! From my night at Tom's house! Tom had said he would take care of it. Had he forgotten?

The lies came effortlessly. "No, Mami, don't get mad, it's nothing. I didn't want to tell you because it was just a parking ticket. When you went to Yosemite, I spent the night at Liz's house and I didn't know you couldn't park on the street in her neighborhood. So the next morning when I drove home I saw the ticket on my windshield. I just went to the post office, bought a money order and mailed it with the citation. I swear. I paid for it. I don't know why they sent a notice when I've already paid for it!"

My mom handed me the folded summons. "Isabel, they wouldn't send this if you've already paid for the ticket. Now you've been fined for not paying. This $50 is coming out of your next allowance, you hear me?"

"Okay, Mami, that's fine. I promise I was trying to be responsible. Maybe I just didn't send the money order correctly. It was the first time I ever filled one out. I don't know."

My mother turned and began to walk toward the front porch. She looked back and said, "Isabel, the next time you get a ticket, you'd better tell me!"

"Yes, Mami," I shouted back as she disappeared through the front door.

I was too embarrassed to call Tom and ask him about the parking ticket he had snatched off my windshield over a month ago. I was just relieved that my mother hadn't investigated the ticket to find out it was actually issued in a different part of town than where Liz lived. Deep inside, I was also relieved to find that it had been a parking ticket, rather than one of Tom's love letters.

Chapter Twenty-One

It's the End of the World as We Know It

After several years of secrecy, sneaking around, lying, cheating, longing, jealousy, and intimacy, my clandestine love affair with Tom suffered an unexpected and severe setback, just weeks before my high school graduation.

"Isabel, I need to speak with you *today*," Tom whispered nervously in my ear. He was standing next to me while I fumbled through the books in my locker. "Danielle was the one who picked up the phone last night while we were talking. She noticed I was out in the garage on the cordless phone at midnight, so she picked up the phone in the house and heard your voice. I don't know if she heard more than she's willing to admit, but it got pretty messy."

I didn't need Tom to recount what had occurred; I had come to those conclusions on my own after I heard the *click* while we were on the phone the previous night. Senior year had gone so smoothly, without any hiccups, rumors, close calls, or obstacles for us. No one at school except Liz knew what was going on between Tom and me, and we had continued seeing each other off-campus without a hitch. We'd just been extremely careful. After I turned seventeen, Tom felt more comfortable in our relationship. He'd told me that I was almost legal, and that soon he wouldn't have to worry anymore.

He'd never said anything about leaving his wife for me, but I'd found ways to avoid thinking about that, and I'd started to look at my options. My body had matured in the last years, my curves becoming more prominent. My hips had rounded out, my breasts became fuller, and my face took on a more chiseled appearance. I began to shape my eyebrows with tweezers, and even highlighted my long brown hair with honey-colored streaks. Tom wasn't the only man looking at me these days, and I already had plans to leave for college over the summer. It wasn't that I didn't love him anymore, but I'd realized that he might not be the last man I loved. And I wasn't willing to put my life on hold for him, seeing that his situation at home was unlikely to change.

A small part of me was glad that his wife had picked up the phone. A larger part of me thought that it was about time we had this conversation, and came to a conclusion about what to do. Not right now, though; I was on my way to class, and the last thing I wanted to do was have a discussion with Tom about the consequences of our careless actions in a place as public as the hallway. In fact, my plan was to ignore him at all costs. I had talked to Liz about the situation earlier, and had already decided that this was going to be the breaking point. He was right; I was almost legal now, and there was no reason to keep our relationship a secret anymore. This was the perfect accident, and the right time for him to man up. I was going to break up with him, and I'd decided to end it today, unless he agreed to leave his wife and take our relationship to another level. I didn't expect him to make this decision easily, but I was tired of playing second fiddle and having to hide.

"I really can't, Tom," I muttered. "I have a lot to do before graduation, and I don't really want to get involved in anything between you and your wife." I moved a step to the side, pulling away from him. "It sounds to me like you got caught, and it's time for you to make some tough decisions. Now's your chance." I looked expectantly at him, hoping he'd get the message.

"Isabel, please don't pull away from me now," he said, stepping closer to me. "Not when I need you most."

"Look," I started, "You don't need this secrecy in your life, and neither do I. It's time for you to decide what you're going to do. Do you love me or do you love your wife? If you care about your marriage and you want to save it, then I don't want to be involved. If you care about me more, then we can talk." I had thought about this entire situation all night long. I couldn't sleep after Tom hung up the phone unexpectedly and I knew that this would be a turning point in our relationship. All night long I tossed and turned, reliving the years of love and heartache, the jealousy, the excitement, the disappointments, and the hope of one day having Tom the right way. Naively, for years, I had hoped Tom would love me enough to leave his wife and commit to me, perhaps after graduation. But I was beginning to think that would never happen, and the way he was protecting his wife from our affair was proof of that. A surge of confidence flowed through me, and I could finally speak the things I had kept to myself for so long.

Tom stared at me, taken aback. The lines around his eyes looked deeper than ever, and his hazel eyes were no longer bright with joy, but shrouded with stress and fatigue. His mouth turned down in disappointment and confusion.

"Isabel, just give me an hour, I need to speak with you alone," he said. "Please? That's all I'm asking. I don't know what I'm going to do, I haven't even thought about it yet. But I must talk to you."

His voice was defeated, and the concern in his eyes was heartbreaking. He looked so tired and forlorn standing there, the charm gone from his voice and demeanor. My heart softened for a moment as I tried to remember the man I had fallen in love with. Was I making a mistake? I wondered. Was I reacting too strongly?

Then I remembered the conversation I had had with Liz that morning, and my resolve returned. This was what I had to do, I reminded myself. This was the best thing for me. I took a long breath before responding, doing my best to keep my voice from quivering.

"No, Tom, there's nothing left to say. I'm sorry but I've made up my mind. I'm leaving for college soon, your wife's onto you, and that's the end of it. Either you make a change or you don't. If you don't…"

I let my voice trail off, but my intention was clear; it was going to be her or me, finally. Shutting my rickety locker door, I turned my back on the man I loved and walked away as quickly as my legs would allow. By the time I reached the other end of campus, tears were streaming uncontrollably down my cheeks. The girls' restroom down the hall from my class would be my sanctuary; the dark, cold room would witness my desperate breakdown.

I somehow managed to make it through the rest of the school day without falling victim to another of Tom's confrontations. I laid low and went to all of my classes, avoiding his side of campus. I asked Liz to watch out for him when we were together, and warn me if she saw him nearby. When the last bell rang, I headed quickly to my locker. I watched him out of the corner of my eye as I rummaged through my stuff, and saw him say goodbye to some of his students. When he turned my way, I shut my locker and practically sprinted down the crowded hall, across the parking lot, and to my car.

I drove on autopilot. When I finally got to the last traffic light, just blocks away from my house, I noticed the large truck idling behind me and did a double take. I hadn't been paying attention to the cars around me as I drove, and seeing Tom's truck behind me almost made me drive off the road. He was behind the wheel, as I knew he would be, and he looked incredibly upset. My heart began to race. I didn't believe that he just happened to be going in my direction; I knew from experience that he lived in the opposite direction, and didn't have friends on this side of town.

The red arrow on the traffic signal turned green, and I turned my car and raced down the narrow street. Behind me, Tom turned and followed me closely. What was he thinking? I panicked as I realized that he meant to follow me home. I couldn't allow him to come to my house; my parents would ask so many questions. I put my foot on the accelerator and sped ahead, trying to lose Tom, but he continued to tail me.

I looked in the rear view mirror again, considering my options. Tom clearly intended to follow me all the way home in his determination to speak to me. I didn't think I had much choice; he was risking everything to talk to me. He'd already been caught once, and he evidently was not afraid of getting caught again. I had to play his game, at least for the afternoon. My heart pounded loudly in my chest as I made my decision, finally easing off the accelerator and driving out of my neighborhood. I needed to find a neutral location, where Tom could park and approach me.

I drove to a neighboring town where Tom and I had met when we didn't have enough time to meet at the foothills. Tom must have known exactly where I was going, because he accelerated and overtook me. By the time I turned into the empty alleyway, he had already parked his truck and was leaning against the passenger door waiting for me. I glanced at him, then down the deserted alleyway. I had trusted this man once, but his actions today made me nervous, and I wondered what exactly he had planned.

I pulled forward and parked, watching him stride quickly toward the passenger door of my car. I'd never seen Tom move so quickly or aggressively, and his eyes had taken on a bright, fevered look. He didn't look like the man I'd loved for so long. He opened the passenger door and jumped into the seat next to me, locking his door. As if locking the passenger door were not enough to startle me, he reached over and locked my door as well. I looked at him, confused. Did he think he was holding me hostage or something? What had gotten into this man? In the three years we had loved each other, I had never once felt physically threatened or intimidated by him. But today, there was desperation in his eyes and his body language was, for the first time, jerky and unrecognizable.

His words affirmed this thought. "Isabel, please look at me. You can't do this! You can't just decide that it's over!" He paused and closed his eyes, trying to gain control of his voice. "That's not how this works. You're my life and I can't just lose you like this."

His eyes burned a hole through my heart, my body becoming rigid. I couldn't speak nor face him, and I didn't want to see the sorrow in his eyes. I had known that this would hurt him, but I hadn't thought it would be this emotional. And I hadn't realized that it would hurt me as well. Suddenly his hand came to my face to grasp my chin. He raised my face so that his eyes could meet mine.

"Isabel, please look at me!"

I took a breath to steady myself and looked up at him. I began to speak slowly, hoping that he would look past his anger and hear what I was about to say.

"Tom, you need to settle down and listen to me. We can't do this anymore. I can't play second fiddle to your wife anymore, and I'm not going to ruin your marriage either. This can't be my burden. I can't take it anymore! Can't you understand that? Why do you want to take more chances? Doesn't your wife know? How can you keep lying to her, hoping to get away with this? And what did you think would happen? Did you think that we'd always be together, that I'd always be willing to take the back seat to your marriage? I just . . . I just can't do this anymore. It hurts too much. I'm sorry."

Tom's body language changed; he relaxed the firm grip he had on my jaw and his eyes lost their look of confusion. His voice took on the charming, coaxing tone I knew so well.

"When I talked to her today, I convinced Danielle that you were one of my students calling because of a personal crisis," Tom told me. "Danielle didn't actually hear anything incriminating, she just heard a girl's voice and that's when I hung up. So she's got no real proof. You don't have to worry. Anyway, I convinced her that it was innocent … just me trying to be there for one of my students. So there's nothing to worry about, Isabel, you didn't ruin anything! You have to believe me. Things are okay, I promise. You just can't leave me now. Please, Isabel, you're my whole world."

"But, that's not enough," I said, my voice trembling. "That means that you're still trying to mend things with her, still trying to keep me a secret, and I just can't take that anymore. Maybe it didn't hit me before, but after last night, reality just smacked me on the face. I can't be part of this, it's not fair to me." I straightened my spine, hoping to bolster my conviction. This was what I had already decided, I reminded myself. This was what was right for me, and I had to stand up for myself. I had to finally do what was right for Isabel, rather than allowing him to talk me into ignoring the reality of our relationship.

"Isabel, I need to tell you something," Tom said intensely, "I need you to know exactly why I got married. It's not what you think. I've never told you because I'm ashamed of it, and I didn't want you to think less of me. I proposed to Danielle on a night that I don't even remember. I was high on drugs and drunk at the time. We were so young, and I was stupid, doing stupid things. But I was never in love with her, and I'm not in love with her now. It was the stupidest thing I've ever done. After I woke up the next morning, I didn't have the guts to back out of the engagement or the wedding. I was a coward then, and I've always regretted it. I don't love her, Isabel. When I tell you that you're it, it's coming from my heart. I love *you*. It's that simple. You're the one I've been waiting for my entire life, and I just can't let you go, Isabel. I need you."

My mind spun. I didn't know what to think. Was he making this up to keep me? Was he really that desperate? It was impossible for me to imagine him high on drugs or even drunk. The thought of Tom high on drugs made me incredibly sad and I felt discouraged.

"Isabel," Tom whispered, "you're the only thing in my life that makes sense. I didn't want kids, I didn't want the marriage that I ended up with. I'm unhappy and trapped. But I don't know if I can leave her or the kids. Please, you have to understand how hard this is for me."

I'm not sure if Tom read the hurt look on my face, but inside of me the sadness turned to confusion. I had told him exactly what he needed to do to keep me, and he was refusing to hear it. Did he actually think that he could talk his way out of this? Talk me into continuing a dead-end relationship with him? If he did, he was wrong. I was stronger now, and after today I felt stronger than him, emotionally. I began to pull away, searching for a way to get him out of the car. Tom continued to talk, explaining what had gone on in the marriage, and how he'd been forced into one adult decision after another at a young age. Every word seemed to hurt me even more, and I did not want to hear about his marriage anymore. The drug and alcohol admission was one thing, but to hear him trying to validate his reasons for staying with his family, after I'd specifically told him that I could no longer deal with the kind of relationship we had …

"You need to stop," the words spilled out of my mouth. "I can't put myself through this anymore. First, it hasn't been fair to your family. Now, though, I have to think of myself. I've had a lot of chances in the last couple years – chances to be with guys, or to go places, or to lead a normal life. And you know what? I didn't take them, because I felt like I would be cheating on you. I couldn't even get through a first kiss with another guy because of how committed I was to you. I couldn't take trips with my friends because I knew that you would miss me too much. I spent my entire high school career terrified of the teachers and students around me, just so I could continue to see you. I love you, but it's just not fair to me. If you love me as much as you say you do, you should understand that. Is that too much to ask, Tom?" By the time I finished speaking, I felt as though I had been shouting. I took a deep breath, trying to calm myself, but the damage was done. I was hurt and disappointed, and my mind was firmer than ever. I was leaving him. Now.

"Are you serious?" he demanded with a frown etched onto his face. "You're just going to turn your back on me, just like that? After all I've sacrificed for you? Isabel, please! Just take some time to think about it before you make a rash decision. No one can love you more than I do; I don't even know if that's humanly possible. Please, Isabel, I know you love me!"

Tom's desperation was increasing, and I knew I had to get him out of my car before something happened. My parents were expecting me home, and I was afraid that Tom, who was clearly not listening to reason, might do something foolish.

"Okay look, I need to get home," I told him quietly. "Let's just meet this weekend, okay? After we've both had some time to think. That way we can have more time to talk, in the comfort of your truck, up in the mountains. My parents expected me home more than half an hour ago, and I don't want them to be suspicious. Please?"

Tom reached over and pulled my face close to his, so that our foreheads met. "You're my sweetheart, Isabel. You mean everything to me. You know that, don't you?"

I managed a forced smile and a reply. "Yeah, I do."

I gently nudged him from my car, and drove away as quickly as I could, frustrated tears rolling down my cheeks.

Chapter Twenty-Two

With or Without You

The weekend came and went without the romantic rendezvous I had promised Tom. I stayed home from school for the last two days of the week to avoid him. He called on Thursday, on Friday (twice), and on Saturday morning (four times). I asked my mom to tell any guy that called that I was not home.

"Why are you so rude to boys?" my mother wanted to know. "One day, you're going to really like a boy and he's not going to take your calls. Let's see how you feel then."

I rolled my eyes. As much as my mother fought with me about "being rude to boys," she always played the game; she answered phones and told them I wasn't around. Maybe in the back of her mind she thought that she was protecting me, and I was allowing her to.

I decided to stay home for the weekend as well; I didn't know what Tom might try when he realized I was blowing him off. No matter how hurt, I did not expect Tom to make an unwise decision and show up at my front door. He would be risking way too much, so I felt safe at home.

On Sunday evening, my mom handed me a sealed envelope and said, "Here Isabel, I forgot to give this to you, it came in the mail yesterday morning." The envelope was crisp and white with neat handwriting on the front.

"Thanks, mami," I said taking the envelope from her with caution. My mom walked out of my room just as swiftly as she had walked in, showing no curiosity about the envelope that had just arrived. I gently peeled it open searching for signs of tampering at the seal, but it was intact. Feeling assured that I was the first one to be reading the contents; I unfolded the letter and immediately recognized Tom's handwriting.

July 14, 1995

Dear Isabel,

Isabel, I realize you've decided to ignore me again. I don't think I have to tell you how much this breaks my heart. But then again, you're still young and behaving as any teenage girl might, so how can I be upset with you? This is your first adult relationship. As you will find out in life, adults don't blow each other off, they don't ignore each other, and they don't trash relationships on a whim. I'm disappointed and hurt. Why now? Why like this? You graduate in one week, Isabel! After that, I may never see you again. You love me, don't you? If you love me still, why don't you at least respect me enough to end things in person? To allow me to hold you, to kiss you one last time.

I thought that our love could keep us together under difficult circumstances, just as it did for the last three years. Isn't that what you told me, just the other night? Or do you not love me anymore? Is there someone else?

I hope you'll make the right decision and respect my love for you. Don't forget, I've done nothing but love you and all I want is a final goodbye, if this is how it has to be. If you want to end this then at least give me one last time to hold you … that's all I ask.

I wanted to tell you that I have made a decision about my wife, and my marriage, but I'd rather tell you in person. Please, please meet with me, one last time.

I hope to hear from you.

Love,

Tom

P.S. Just as before, please make sure to destroy this letter after you've read it.

I went back to school on Monday, to try to enjoy my last week of high school. Tom made every excuse to get near me, but Liz acted as my bodyguard, shielding me from Tom at every turn. She even walked with me to our shared locker between periods to make sure that Tom could not approach me in private. After school, she rode home with me. We went to her house every day, rather than mine, and stayed there until dark. Tom almost inevitably followed, but by the time I drove home at 6:00 or 7:00 in the evening, he'd left to go home to his family. I took this as a sign that he'd made his decision, and renewed my dedication to ignore him. I didn't plan to give him the "one last time" he'd asked for. As far as I was concerned, it was already over.

I dreaded the night of my high school graduation as it represented an end to many good years of exploration and discovery, but found the atmosphere pleasantly festive. I sat on the grassy lawn wearing a white honor-roll robe, surrounded by good friends. We all managed to giggle as jokes spread from ear to ear and pass notes during the long and boring speeches. I looked up at one point from the note that Liz had written me, and scanned the row of teachers, then the crowd. Tom was somewhere in the crowd, I knew. Maybe he had brought his wife and kids with him to the graduation. I thought about the pain I had inflicted on him and couldn't help but wonder whether I had been too callous in ending things. No matter how many times I thought about it, though, I couldn't see any other way to handle it. And I knew for a fact that if I was going to end it, the only way to do so was to leave without saying goodbye. It had worked before, and I was convinced it would work again.

Liz glanced over at me, saw me staring at the crowd, and elbowed me in the ribs. "Stop thinking about him," she lectured. "You did what had to be done. Now move on. Grow up. Live your life."

I smiled and nodded, knowing that she was right. I had tried to be honest; I had even tried to invoke his love for me as a reason why he should let me go. I had tried asking him to leave his wife for me, to get me to stay. Nothing had worked. He hadn't wanted to listen to reason, and it was his own fault that I had to walk away from him, from our relationship. We shared equal guilt for the relationship itself, but at least I could take responsibility for the break-up.

After the ceremony concluded, our families and friends flooded the field. The air smelled of freshly cut flowers and popcorn, and the graduates scattered, looking for their families. From afar, it must have looked like a swarm of colorful ants heading for fallen cookie crumbs. I dragged Liz with me to find my parents, telling her that we'd find hers afterwards. We'd gone only 10 feet when I felt eyes on me. I turned, glancing through the crowd to find Tom standing behind the row of chairs in front of us, staring at me. He was standing with several other teachers. They were talking, but he had moved aside to stare at me as I passed, his eyes burning with pain and questions.

Time froze. The rush of people around me faded into the periphery. For the next fifteen seconds, only Tom and I existed. Then his wife walked up behind him and put her hand on his arm. As much as it pained me to cut him out of my life, I knew at that moment that if I wanted to live a normal life, I had to walk away.

Breaking the stare, I looked down to study the grass around my feet. I swallowed deeply and felt Liz's hand on my arm, giving me comfort and support. Then I looked back up at Tom. *It's over*, I told him with my eyes.

I turned away, and before I knew it, my legs were striding confidently away from Tom, away from the relationship we once shared.

Chapter Twenty-Three
Please, Please Tell Me Why?

I started packing my things the next day. I was due to leave in August, but wanted to get a head start on the painful task of gathering my life and shipping it somewhere else. It also gave me something to do. Although it had been my decision to end things with Tom, despair and sadness filled my heart, along with a heavy dose of guilt. I had grown especially attached to this man, who had played the part of a fairytale prince in my life for three years, and I wasn't positive that I had done the right thing. I questioned my decision, my actions, and even my mind for an entire night. When I woke up, I decided that the only way to stop thinking about it was to keep busy.

The weeks that followed graduation day were the most difficult of my life. Mornings were especially grueling. My mind wandered every night, and my dreams reconnected me with Tom, as if the relationship had never ended. I saw his truck in town during the day, but always turned and walked away. The reality of the situation was that Tom was no longer in my life. He had made his decision and stayed with his wife. In my heart, I knew there was no going back. And Tom never called again.

I dove headfirst into my studies at college to distract myself from Tom. I ignored the parties, people, and interested guys, and focused only on being the best in my classes. Many of the people around me tried to make friends and ask me out, but I simply wasn't interested. My heart had been broken - badly - and I wasn't going to give it away again. At least not right now. I didn't believe that I could fall for anyone as deeply as I had fallen for Tom, and ending that relationship had torn my heart to pieces. My books and grades were steady and dependable, and they never hurt me the way that other people could.

At the end of my first year in college, I decided to take a trip home before heading to Washington D.C. for a prestigious summer internship. I missed my parents and brother, and wanted to see my old friends again. My parents had moved out of Hillside to a more upscale community in the next valley, and now owned a larger house and more land.

I'd heard about the new house, but was surprised when I arrived; it was larger than any other house on the block, and gave my mother plenty of room to run her successful business.

"We would have killed for a house this big when we were young!" I joked with Tony, who had come home to see me. Tony had married Amy several months earlier, though I hadn't come for the wedding, and lived in Hillside in my parents' old rental house. They saw each other often, I knew, and Tony had become especially close to my father.

He laughed, nodding, and pulled me out the door. "You have to see the pool in the back! It would have come in handy when you were on the swim team."

I followed him outside, agreeing, and strode toward the large, decorative pool deck. The site of the water brought a rush of memory with it, and I gasped. The East Coast didn't have the weather for year-round swimming, and I hadn't been around a pool since high school. The smell of the chlorine, and sight of the bright, sparkling water, took me immediately back to the Royal Oaks pool, and a range of emotions that I'd spent a year avoiding. I was relieved when my mom called to me from the house.

"Isabel! You have a phone call," she called, holding the phone before her.

I walked into the house and approached my mom, who extended the receiver out to me. "Who on earth knows I'm home?"

My mom shrugged. "It's Vicky."

I grinned, surprised, and took the phone. "Vicky? Seriously?"

The swim champion from my high school team, and dear friend, laughed on the other end of the line. "Hey, Isabel, I heard you were home! My sister ran into your parents last weekend at the mall and they said you were going to be here. Let's hang out before you leave for D.C.! It's been forever since we've seen each other. I'm the new head coach for the swim team at Royal Oaks, and I've got practice tomorrow morning. Remember Mrs. Robbins, the assistant coach while we were on the swim team, who hated us so much? She's now *my* assistant. Isn't that funny? Anyway, I've got practice from ten to noon, so why don't you just come by the school? I'm sure you'll recognize some of the swimmers, because some of them were freshmen and sophomores when we were seniors on the team. We can hang out during practice."

I smiled into the phone and listened to Vicky chatter on. I had forgotten that she carried on entire conversations by herself, and expected everyone to agree to whatever she set up. It would be good to see her. The thought of being back on that campus, though, made my stomach turn. The Royal Oaks campus had been my romantic playground and the backdrop of so much drama and despair. Every inch of that campus reminded me of Tom; in fact, it was as though I had no other memories of that place. I gulped at the thought, and asked aloud if there were any other place we could meet. Vicky told me absolutely not, though, and insisted on me coming to our old stomping grounds at the pool.

I sighed at her response. I wasn't prepared to see Tom face to face; in fact, for the sake of my healing heart, I hoped never to see him again. I'd spent the last year trying to forget him, and trying to numb the pain in my heart. If I'd been a different person, perhaps I would have come home sooner, to try to mend things with him. But I'd made my decision, and I didn't think I would have another chance to renew the relationship. Maybe this would be my opportunity to let go of what happened, I thought, and to prove to myself that I had finally moved on. I was a grown woman now, and I needed to face the emotions that burdened me. How many times had my friends told me that I had to face things before I could move on and get over them?

I agreed to meet Vicky, my heart pounding, and hung up the phone. It was summer, after all, I thought. What were the chances of Tom even being on campus?

The school hadn't changed. The campus was still decrepit and poorly maintained. The buildings looked smaller than they had, though, and dingier. I sighed at the thought, glad that I didn't have to come here every day anymore, and parked my mother's new BMW convertible – which she had allowed me to drive – in the parking lot near the swimming pool. As I pulled the parking brake, something caught my attention, and I looked up. Tom's conspicuous truck was parked at the far end of the lot.

My mind catapulted, while my heart dropped into my stomach. The first shock came when I realized that Tom was, in fact, on campus at that moment. That thought led to an immediate flood of questions. Tom never parked his truck in the student parking lot. Why had he done so today? Did he know I was going to be stopping by? Who would have told him, and why? Certainly not Vicky. Why was the truck parked so close to the edge of the parking lot, near the street exit? Tom always parked his truck as close to his classroom as possible, so what was it doing parked at the very edge today?

My mind paused on the final, most important question. Where, exactly, was he? Was it safe to get out of the car, or would I run into him as soon as I turned the corner?

I finally talked myself into believing that he would be in class or otherwise occupied, and jumped out of the car. The short walk from where I had parked my mother's car to the swimming pool felt like it took hours, though I was practically sprinting. Behind me, just meters away, was the threatening presence of Tom's truck, and all around me was the possibility of seeing him again. When I reached the pool, though, I found only Vicky's smiling face. I ducked through the gate and behind a building, breathing a sigh of relief.

"Hey, I've been waiting for you!" Vicky hollered when she saw me walk through the rusted chain-link gate. She looked exactly the same, except for her hair, which was longer – almost down to her waist. "Look, Isabel, do you remember some of these guys? They were on the team when we were swimmers two years ago, remember?"

I nodded, glancing at the kids in the pool. "How on earth did you end up being the head swim coach?" I asked, walking with her toward the all-too-familiar concrete benches. "What happened to Mr. Stevens?"

Vicky frowned and shook her head. "The principal kicked him out of the position when he was investigated, you know that story. He never got the job back." She shrugged and smiled. "Besides, I was the star of the team! I make a way better coach than he ever did!"

Vicky leaned closer to me, making sure no one else could overhear what she was about to say. "Actually, I've heard some of the swimmers say that Mr. Stevens is doing it again. You know, having a thing with one of the sophomores in his class. What's her name? I think it was Christy, or something like that. Maybe Kristen, I don't know. Apparently she's a blonde cheerleader. They're seen together all the time, and they've even been seen leaving campus together. Can you believe it? Principal Warren can't really do anything about it because who knows if it's really true. I mean last time Mr. Stevens got reported, look what happened. No truth, all rumors, or so they say. No one ever testified, and the police never found anything against him. Go figure. Anyway, I don't think he's interested in coaching the swim team anymore."

I'm not sure if Vicky noticed the look on my face, but I felt like a jagged wound had been viciously ripped open in my heart. Tom was fooling around with another student? Already? After all we had been through together, and all the things he'd said to me? I wanted to scream, though I swallowed hard and tried to look unconcerned. He had told me that he loved me, and that I was the only one for him. I had given him my heart and my virginity. I felt like the air had been kicked out of me.

As Vicky's voice droned on, I tried to calm myself. *Isabel, stop freaking out! They were probably rumors. You know how high school kids can be, gossiping at every turn. Some students probably saw him being friendly to this cheerleader, and they jumped to conclusions. That's it. Yeah, that's it. He isn't with anyone else.*

Another voice chimed in, though, and said things that I didn't want to hear. What if this was his MO? What if he started things with girls, maintained them, and then moved on when the girls went to college?

That thought led to another, more painful one. If I wasn't the last, and he'd moved on already … did that mean that I also hadn't been the first?

"Isabel, are you listening to me?"

"Oh, sorry Vicky. I was just thinking about all the stuff I have to get done before heading to D.C. - sorry. What did you say?"

"I just said that I can end practice a little early, so we can head to lunch." She got up from the bench and turned back toward me. "Why don't you head to In N' Out now, just in case there's a line? You can hold a table for us. I'll close up here and meet you there in fifteen minutes. I have to get the kids out of the pool and lock the gate."

I nodded, realizing that I was famished. The drive and the wait would also give me some time to get myself together and put on a happier face. "You got it. I'll see you at In N' Out in a little while."

Wanting nothing more than to leave, I jumped up and made my way to the gate. As I walked quickly toward my mother's car, staring down at the concrete in contemplation, something compelled me to look up toward the parking lot. The lot was still empty, but in the far corner something stirred. Something almost out of sight.

It was a shadow near Tom's truck. There was movement there; something was going on. I crouched down a bit and walked more quickly toward the BMW, hoping to avoid detection. The last thing I needed was a confrontation; I was already too emotional over what I'd just heard, and seeing Tom would just make it worse. I jumped into the car and locked the doors behind me, crouching low so I wouldn't be seen. After a few moments, I peeked up over the dashboard.

Tom was inside his truck, which had been home to many hours of our lovemaking. Next to him was a petite blonde girl, half-hidden from view. The blonde figure seemed to shift closer to Tom, and then, before I knew it, the truck was driving off.

A sharp pain shot through my chest, and I failed to breathe. Moments after watching Tom drive away with his new girl, I broke down, sobbing, full of revulsion and heartbreak. Every last inch of my body felt the loss. I had ended the relationship, and it had broken my heart to turn my back on him, but that had been different; that breakup had been on *my* terms. This feeling of being replaced was utterly heart wrenching. I was powerless against the wave of emotion that rushed over me.

For the first time in my life, I felt truly and wholeheartedly deceived. I had known that I still loved Tom, and missed him, but I hadn't realized how deep that love still went. And with one simple stroke, one terrible decision, Tom had ripped the love out of my heart and sent me plummeting down an endless chasm of pain. How could he do this to me? After all I had given him! My love, my devotion, my virginity! The most meaningful years of my life! All I could hear in my head, over and over again, was one phrase: please, please tell me why?

Chapter Twenty-Four

You Were Meant for Me

I went to lunch with Vicky, and did my best to act as though nothing were wrong. We chatted about high school and college, our friends - both new and old - and what we planned to do with our futures. I told her about my internship in Washington, D.C., and the direction I was leaning toward for a career. By the end of the meal I was exhausted from maintaining the mask of happiness and excitement. I drove away from the restaurant with a promise that we would go see a movie later, and her number in my planner.

When I got home, I rushed past my mother and went straight to my room, where I'd unpacked my things for the few weeks I was planning on staying. I'd learned some things about myself at college, and I knew now that the letters to Tom had started something in me – a craving for the written word, and a feeling that writing things down would allow me to let go of them. I walked quickly toward my desk, pushed some of the clutter onto the floor, and pulled out my latest diary and favorite pen. The diary fell open to the last page I'd written, and I stared at the next page, my mind refusing to move forward. Finally I put the pen to the paper to write the date and my standard opening. Words and phrases began to flow out of me, and before I knew it I had written five pages. I read back through the writing and saw many things – the rejection I felt, the shock and horror at Tom's actions, a lasting feeling of having been taken advantage of, and the disappointment of finding someone I loved to be less than what I thought he was.

Under it all laid my broken heart and the knowledge that I had never really let go of him. I reached down and wrote one final line: "I didn't realize it at the time, but I believe now that I came home with the idea of making up with him." The petite blonde girl in his truck made that impossible, I thought, sitting back in my chair.

I turned to stare out the window at the pool below me, thinking about all that had happened and all of the possibilities for the future. I felt drained and exhausted, the emotions wrung from me by the writing, but I hadn't come up with a plan. I didn't know my direction. And I knew myself well enough to know that I needed one.

"What are you going to do?" Liz asked quietly. I'd done what I would have done in high school – called my best friend. She was the only one that knew about my relationship with Tom, and the only one I trusted. She was also the only person who could listen to my story and give me sincere advice.

I frowned. "I'm not sure, Liz," I answered. "I'm pulled in two completely different directions, here. One part of me wants to run away, heartbroken, and forget all about this place. I don't want to see or think about him ever again." I paused, thinking.

"And the other?" she asked.

I looked up, shrugging. "The other part of me wants to act like an adult. Like the people around me would have acted if they'd known what was going on when we were in high school. If he's taking advantage of another girl – if he's doing with her what he did with me – someone should tell the police. Or her parents. Or something."

Liz snorted with laughter. "And I suppose the fact that doing so would get him in trouble – probably arrested, and kicked out of teaching for good – would help your broken heart. Just a little."

I smiled, unable to resist her sarcastic humor, and nodded. "I suppose that's part of it, too," I admitted. "I just don't know how I would do it, though. I don't know if I *can* do it."

Liz pulled a paper napkin toward her, and pulled out a ballpoint pen. "The way I see it," she muttered, "you have a

couple of options. Let's just say that you're going to tell someone about it. The first, most obvious move would be to talk to
the girl. See if you can talk some sense into her. If that doesn't
work, you could go to her parents. And if *that* doesn't work
– though I don't know why it wouldn't – you could go to the
police. You could either tell them what he's doing with the
girl, or you could tell them what he did with you." She looked
up from her notes and caught my eye. "I'm sure they still have
a file on you. People watch him pretty closely, you know."

I nodded, thinking. I did have the power to put Tom behind
bars, if I wanted. It would never have occurred to me before,
but I hated the thought that he was doing this to another girl.
If I was being honest with myself, I was heartbroken over it,
and the idea of retribution was far outweighing the noble act
of protecting someone. Whether I could actually go through
with it or not, though – tell the police, get him arrested, possibly ruin his life …"The girl first, then," I said quickly, making my decision. "If she'll listen to me, it puts the situation in
her hands, and then it's her problem. Maybe I won't have to be
involved any more than that."

I spent the whole night coming up with a plan, and went back
and forth at least a hundred times. My heart was pounding
the entire time; confronting this girl meant that I would have
to hear – from her mouth – that she and Tom were having a
relationship. I had no doubt that he'd told her the same things
that he'd told me; that he was in love with her, that she was

the only one for him, that he didn't love his wife, and that he couldn't live without her. I didn't doubt either that she would repeat all of these things to me. I remembered being fifteen, and knew how she would view me. I would be practically an old woman to her, and she would think that I had no idea what I was talking about. She would be convinced that I couldn't understand how she was feeling, or what she and Tom had.

She won't believe that I had a relationship with him too, I thought finally, that truth hurting worse than the others had.

I would have to find a way to convince her, and use words firm enough to encourage her to find help rather than keeping quiet. I would have to tell her about our relationship, and use information that I'd never given anyone about Tom. If she wouldn't listen, I would have to tell her that I was going to go to her parents, and perhaps the police.

I swallowed heavily, wondering if I was ready to do that. I had been crying for hours, and my eyes were sore and puffy. My throat was raw from my sobs, and I didn't think I'd have much of a voice tomorrow. My heart had become a deep, dark place, full of pain and sorrow. But I couldn't deny what was going on, and I had to admit to myself that the direction was giving me some comfort. I had searched my heart and didn't believe that I was doing this to hurt Tom. In my subconscious, though, sat the idea that if I couldn't have him, no one was going to.

By the time I went to bed, I had a plan.

I drove to the school the next morning, before classes started. The plan was simple: walk around the campus while students found their way to their classes, look for the girl in question, and find out who she was. I realized that it might not be that easy, but it was a small school and I had graduated only a year earlier; there were plenty of people who still remembered me. This was summer term, so there would be even fewer students, though I knew – from having seen her yesterday – that the girl I was searching for was here.

My heart raced as I parked in the student lot and walked toward the campus. The students milled around me, uncaring, and I thought that I would probably still blend in fairly effectively. That didn't change the fact that I was on campus at the same time as Tom. I knew he was here – I'd seen his truck in the faculty parking lot. He must be teaching another summer class, and with the limited number of students on campus…

Don't think about it, I told myself. After all, I knew where his classroom was – surely he had the same one – and I could avoid that side of campus. I wasn't planning on going into any faculty areas, in any case, and I could duck behind a building if I saw him coming. All I needed was to find a place to sit, so I could watch the students walk by and find the girl I was looking for.

I scooted toward a bench at the entrance of the school and pulled out my journal, so I looked like I was busy. I looked down, reading my last passage, and watched the students walk by through the shade of my sunglasses. Some I recognized, some I didn't; there were new freshmen and sophomores, who looked about ten years old to my newly mature eyes. I laughed to myself; when I was that age, I'd been looking at older men, and wishing I was old enough to date someone with facial hair.

When I was that age, I'd started building a plan to entice one of my coaches, so that I *could* date someone that old. And look how that had turned out.

I looked back at my journal, running my eyes over the notes I'd made. I had to get in touch with this girl, somehow, and talk some sense into her. She had to know what I'd gone through, and where she was heading, so she could keep herself out of trouble. I knew that I had deeper, more selfish reasons for my plan - the desire to keep Tom out of trouble, among them - but I was avoiding thinking about them. In fact, I had spent the entire night trying to keep my thoughts off Tom himself. The fact that he was seeing someone else, taking her home, maybe taking her to the places he'd taken me ... I didn't want him with another girl. He had promised me that I was the only one, and seeing him with someone else was more than I could handle. My mind had gone down that road for a few minutes, and I'd pulled it back. The idea was too painful for words, and obsessing about it wasn't going to get me anywhere.

I caught my breath, realizing that I'd been daydreaming, and looked back up at the courtyard in front of me. I'd lost at least five minutes in my thoughts, and the area was beginning to clear. Had the girl walked by? Had I missed her? Was she even on campus this early? I stood as my eyes scanned the yard, searching desperately for a blonde head, but came up empty. The flow of students slowed to a trickle, and then stopped, and my shoulders sagged. It hadn't been a good plan, but it had been the only one I had. I looked across the courtyard once again, hoping for a straggler, then paused and turned my eyes slowly back the way they'd come. Directly across from me, where the buildings began, a set of eyes peered through the blinds of one of the windows.

When the eyes noticed me looking in their direction, the blinds snapped shut.

I frowned, trying to remember what teacher used that classroom. I wasn't familiar with it, but that didn't mean anything; it could be anyone. My breath caught in my throat at that thought. It could be anyone. I was in an empty courtyard, open to anyone's gaze, sitting by myself.

I turned and ran toward my car, my heart pounding in my chest.

Going back to campus was one of the hardest things I'd ever done. I had no idea who'd been watching me through the blinds of the classroom, but I didn't believe that I'd gone unnoticed. And, given my past with the school, I knew that a number of people would be interested in my presence there. I didn't want to get caught, and I certainly didn't want to get into any trouble. I drove back to campus in the afternoon, promising myself that this was the last time I would try. If I didn't find her today, I told myself, I'd abandon the problem and go back to the East Coast.

I parked in the midst of a group of cars and glanced around. The first thing that caught my eye was the big blue truck in the corner. Tom was here, then, and probably waiting for his new girlfriend. I took a deep breath and bit down on my cheek. As much as I hated it, that truck would be the best – and easiest – place to find her. I pulled out my sunglasses and a large magazine, and settled down to wait.

When school got out, the parking lot flooded with students. I peeked over the magazine at the truck, keeping my eyes peeled for the petite blonde girl I'd seen with Tom. They'd driven by me when they left, and I thought that I could identify her fairly easily, given the time. I hoped that she would be alone, and that she would be careless; I had known to stay away from Tom's truck, but she might not realize that she needed to do so.

I was so busy watching the truck and trying to stay hidden that I almost missed the girl entirely. I'd sneezed and looked down for a moment, then looked back up. When my gaze rose above the dashboard, I was looking at the entrance to the school, and saw her. She was very small and very pretty, with the fine, close-set features I would expect to see on a pixie. She looked very young.

Walking next to her was an older woman with the same face. Her mother, I thought, my heart sinking. Then I squared my shoulders. I would have to be subtler than I expected, but her mother should know that there was a teacher to avoid at the school, as well. I jumped out of the car and walked quickly toward them. When I got close enough, I held my hand out in greeting.

"Hi there," I said brightly, hoping that I sounded sincere. "My name's Isabel Cruz. I used to go to school here, and I was on campus the other day to see an old friend." I looked up at the girl's mother, then back to the girl herself. She was much smaller in person than I'd expected, and much cuter. My heart was pounding, and I gulped. Did Tom find her more attractive than me? Did he like her blonde hair, and her small, pixie-like size? Was he telling her that she was the one?

Did he love her?

The older woman was looking at me like I had lost my mind, and I pressed on. "The thing is," I said to her, dropping my voice, "I noticed that your daughter got into Tom Stevens' truck, and I … well, I … "

The woman frowned at me, her face closing. "Yes?" she asked quietly.

I felt my resolve slipping. How was I supposed to say this? "Well, I saw her getting into Tom's truck," I repeated, stuttering a bit. "And I wondered how well you knew him."

The woman frowned at me again, but her daughter cut in. "I've known Mr. Stevens all my life," she said, her voice high and bright. "He's one of Daddy's best friends. He was just giving me a ride home, not that it's any of your business." She shot me a dark glance, and I remembered the feeling of being fifteen and in love. The girl probably felt like she was the most important person in the world.

"Yes, he's a family friend," the woman continued, glancing at her daughter and back at me. "I don't know why you're asking, but my daughter's right – he's one of my husband's best friends. We've known him for years. I work long hours at my job, and he gives my daughter a ride home when I can't make it. He's really quite understanding about it, and since he lost his own kids…"

"What?" I asked, shocked. "His kids? What happened to them?"

The woman looked closely at me, and her frown deepened. "Ms. Cruz, I don't know who you are, or what your relationship is with Tom. I'm not sure that I-"

"Well, that's what I wanted to talk to you about," I broke in, seeing my opportunity. I would ask about Tom's kids later. "You see, I think you need to be careful with your daughter, because-"

"Isabel?" My name cut through the air like a knife and drove directly into my heart. The last words died on my tongue, and I turned slowly to the left.

Tom was standing five feet from us, his face a mask of shock and dismay. His eyes were large and dark, and glassy with unshed tears. Behind the sadness, I saw a glimmer of hope.

"Tom," I sighed. I'd been dreading this meeting, and realized how this must look. I was here talking to the girl he'd started a relationship with. I must represent a world of danger for him – the possibility of another investigation, the potential for discovery. He knew – as I did – that I could turn him in at any moment, or unveil his past to his friends and peers. Our last contact had been so unhappy, and my actions so harsh, that he must have thought that was why I was here. I released the air in my lungs, trying to decide what to do.

My body made the decision for me. I rushed toward him and threw my arms around him, seeking only the support and comfort he'd once given me. His arms came up around me in response to mine, and with them came a flood of memories. This was where I belonged, my body said. This was home, and the safest place in the world.

My brain disagreed, though, and I pulled back. This man was having a relationship with another underage girl, my mind told me, and I had to protect myself. I couldn't fall into his trap again. He released me as quickly as the embrace began.

"Tom," I said, my heart screaming, "it's good to see you, but I have to talk to you. This girl-"

"Oh, you've met Christine," he interrupted, his eyes moving toward the girl and her mother. "Then I'm sure you've also met her mother, Samantha." He glanced back at me, his eyes pleading.

I firmed my mouth, ready to say the words that needed to be said. "Yes, I was just telling them-"

"She says that she knew you when she went to school here, Tom," Samantha interrupted, coming to stand next to us. Her eyes moved from Tom to me and back again, asking silent questions. She raised one eyebrow in his direction. "Is there a problem here?"

Tom shook his head and laughed. "No, no problem at all. Samantha, may I introduce you to Isabel. She was one of the stars of my swim team, back when I coached. I'm sure she's just come by to say hello." He glanced at me again, raising his eyebrows, and I read the mistrust in his eyes. "Samantha and her husband are some of my oldest friends," he said, his voice dropping. "I've known them since college. I often give Christine a ride home when Sam can't make it on time."

I turned back to Samantha, seeking the truth in this statement, and she nodded. My breathing slowed, and I nodded back. Could that be the truth? Could it be as simple as that – giving his friends' daughter a ride home, and nothing more? I looked back at Tom, trying to read him as I once had, and saw his eyes grow clear and friendly. He must have seen me start to believe, because the corner of his mouth turned up and he laughed.

"I'm so sorry, I must have frightened you, coming on like that," I said, turning back to Samantha and her daughter. "I had seen Christine and Tom together, and I thought I could pass a message along." I stopped, my mind racing for an easy excuse. "I didn't think I'd be able to see him, you see. I'm only in town for a short time."

Samantha's face cleared with the excuse, and she gave me a brilliant smile. "Well in that case, I suppose we're all in luck. He's right here, and you can give him your message yourself." She turned back to Tom, shrugging. "I'm afraid we have to be going, though. I'm on my lunch break. Isabel, it was nice to meet you. Tom … give us a call tonight, and let us know that everything's okay." She gave me one last glance, then turned and headed toward her parked car, her daughter in tow. As they were walking away Christine turned back toward us, looking directly at me, and shifting her gaze to Tom. "Oh Mr. Stevens…I forgot to get my necklace from you after cheerleading practice today. Do you have it with you?" Tom stepped toward Christine, fishing her necklace out of his pocket. Christine reached forward to take it from him; in doing so I noticed his hand lingering on her wrist for what felt like an unnecessarily long pause. Tom noticed my piercing inquiry of their exchange and quickly withdrew his hand. As she turned away from Tom's gaze, Christine looked directly at me with a satisfied grin on her face. With a flick of her blond ponytail, she trotted off to catch up with her mother.

I turned back to Tom, wondering how on earth he was going to explain what had just transpired.

Catching me off guard, and dismissing what I had just witnessed, Tom casually teased with a smile on his face, "so, you have a message for me? What on earth could that be?" His hand dropped to his side and flexed, as though he wanted to reach for me again but couldn't bring himself to do so.

I looked down, embarrassed. "Well, the message wasn't really for you. I saw you with Christine yesterday, and I-"

"You thought that I had moved on," Tom finished, reading the truth in my silence.

I nodded miserably, hating the fact that it mattered so much, and after witnessing them together feeling as though my instincts were right.

Suddenly, Tom reached for me and I was in his arms again, pressed against his body and feeling the beat of his heart. "Oh Isabel, did you actually think I would do that?" he whispered, his mouth against my ear, his words sounding insincere. "I could never replace you. You've always been the only one for me."

I leaned against him, finding strength in his presence, and dying to believe him. "It really seems like you've moved on and anyway that doesn't matter because you're still married, you have kids, and there's no way it could have worked out between us," I mumbled, the tears spilling down my face. Suddenly I realized what we were doing – holding each other, in broad daylight, in the middle of the school parking lot – and pulled back. "Don't hold me like that," I said, choking back the tears, "you'll get us in trouble."

He put his hands on my shoulders and held me still so that he could look into my eyes. "Isabel, I left my wife. I couldn't stay with her any longer, knowing what I knew about myself and my feelings. This is what I wanted to tell you I was going to do in the last letter I had written to you. I'm separated now. I've been dreaming of you for a year and praying that you'd come back to me," his mouth grinning as he paused for a moment, "let them see! You're nineteen now, if my math is correct, and it's perfectly legal for me to hug you in a parking lot."

I found myself back under Tom's spell, my mind racing in a million different directions. "But I still have so many unanswered questions, and so much time has passed—"

Tom raised his right hand and put his warm index finger on my lips to silence me. "I promise to answer all of your questions, I've always said you're my one and only. Just say you still love me Isabel, that's all I need to hear."

My heart stopped and it felt like time stood still. I looked directly into Tom's hazel eyes so full of yearning and I knew, in that moment, exactly what I needed to say.

Epilogue

The shocking truth is that relationships between students and teachers exist not only in the U.S. but also across the world. These love affairs may end well, or become tragic, but they all share one common theme: when they become public, they shock the world. The men and women of society react with disgust, surprise, fear, and even anger, judging the adult in the relationship to be a manipulative person, and the student to be the naïve, innocent victim.

These illicit affairs find the same treatment in the courts, where the adult parties are judged guilty of a range of crimes, from sexual molestation to outright rape, sometimes without benefit of an impartial jury. Decisions and judgments are made long before any testimony is heard, and certainly without regard to situation or circumstances. Those teachers lucky enough to avoid jail time must register as sexual offenders, and lose both their jobs and their reputations. They face a future that is dark, grim, and without redemption.

The students find themselves at the other end of the spectrum. They are coddled and treated as victims, handled with kid gloves, and counseled to go on with their lives. They may receive prescriptions for anti-depressants, to allow them to 'forget' what happened to them. They, too, have to deal with the long-term repercussions of the affairs, though – the sideways glances, the asterisks in their records, the knowing looks of those around them.

As we can see, society has already signed and delivered its judgment in cases like these: guilty, regardless of the facts. The world is full of after-school specials about sexual predators and older people who take advantage of adolescents.

But is that always the case? Are these affairs predestined to be manipulative and hurtful, where one party is the abuser and the other the victim? Or is there room for true love in any relationship, regardless of age, circumstance, and context? **Sweetest Taboo** seeks to explore that very idea – that a student and teacher *can* fall in love, share a mutual respect, and even build a life together, despite society's prejudices. This work of fiction takes a new and daring look at the student's side of the story, and reveals that these affairs may in fact find their origin in love, rather than manipulation. Finally, it represents the hope that both parties may go on with their lives, unscarred by the truth of their affairs. Márquez takes a brave and – to some – shocking leap into the realm of fiction and real life, presenting an unsettling fictional memoir, casting both student and teacher in a gentle light, and showing that true love may lie at the base of even the most illicit romance.

Tainted Love

*I*n the second book of the *Sweetest Taboo Series* by Eva Márquez, Isabel thought her life was on track - she was doing well in school, moving quickly toward her future, and deciding who she wanted to be. Best of all, she'd reunited with Tom, the love of her life. But it doesn't take long for her history - and his - to start catching up with them, presenting a range of uncomfortable questions. Does he really love her? Are they meant to be together? And what exactly has he been doing in their time apart?

Visit www.Eva-Marquez.com to read the first two chapters of *Tainted Love*.

Excerpt from *Tainted Love* copyright © 2013 by Eva Márquez.

11788578R00174

Printed in Great Britain
by Amazon.co.uk, Ltd.,
Marston Gate.